Rick
May the peace of Christ
our Lord Jesus the
be with you always
Love
Becky Hussey

Tiramisu

"Lift Me Up"

Becky Hussey

PublishAmerica
Baltimore

© 2007 by Becky Hussey.
All rights reserved. No part of this book may be reproduced, stored in a retrieval system or transmitted in any form or by any means without the prior written permission of the publishers, except by a reviewer who may quote brief passages in a review to be printed in a newspaper, magazine or journal.

First printing

At the specific preference of the author, PublishAmerica allowed this work to remain exactly as the author intended, verbatim, without editorial input.

Scripture text used in this book are taken from the New American Bible, Old Testament of the New American Bible Copyright 1970 by the Confraternity of Christian Doctrine (CCD Washington, DC); Revised New Testament of the New American Bible Copyright 1986 by the Cofraternity of Christian Doctrine, Washington, D.C.; Revised Psalms of the New American Bible, Copyright 1991; Cofraternity of Christian Doctrine, Washington DC. *Used with Permission.*

ISBN: 1-4241-8107-0
PUBLISHED BY PUBLISHAMERICA, LLLP
www.publishamerica.com
Baltimore

Printed in the United States of America

This book is dedicated to Jesus Christ,
my Lord and Savior

Acknowledgements

Heartfelt thanks to my children,
Carissa Marie and Timothy Edmund Hussey for their love,
encouragement and support.

Special thanks to my father, the late George W. Griebel,
my mother, Eleanor Gilson Griebel,
and my sisters, Roberta Griebel and Georgia Gates,
for their ongoing support and inspiration.

Special thanks to my spiritual mothers and sisters for their impartation
of wisdom and their excellent example of Christian love,
Especially: Sister Anna Maria Hartmann and Judi Finkle

Much thanks to my spiritual fathers and brothers for their dedication
to the Lord, Jesus Christ and His teachings especially:
the late Rev. Peter J. Pinto,
the late Rev. Anthony Licastro,
Rev. Michael Bailey,
Rev. Wes Klemmer, Pastor Jorn Junod, and Pastor Ron Neff

Humble thanks and praise to God our Father from whom all good things come.

*"Your servant loves your promise,
it has been proved by fire."*

Psalm 119:140 NAB

Table of Contents

September, 2006

Dear Friends,

I would like to thank you for selecting this book to read. It is my desire to reach out to others in love to share God's message of love and salvation through His son, Jesus Christ. I accepted Jesus as my Lord and Savior when I was a child; however, I really did not understand what this meant until much later. It was not until I stumbled and fell on my walk in life, a number of times, that I began to realize just how much God loves me and what Jesus' death and Resurrection means to me. I am still learning and growing.

God loves you, too! It is my hope than I can help you come to a fuller understanding of what that means and how it can change your life. If you desire a life filled with love and peace, then, this book is written specifically for you.

As you go through the book, I encourage you to take the time to read the scripture references. If you don't have a copy of the Holy Bible, I urge you to invest in one and spend time reading and studying it—daily. I would also like to encourage you to spend time in prayer, speaking to the Lord, often. In any good relationship, there is communication. We must spend time sharing our heart with the Lord as well as listening for his response. No relationship will last very long if one party remains silent or refuses to listen to what the other has to say. The same is true with our prayerful communications.

I am not a pastor or theologian. I'm just an ordinary person sharing what's in my heart. My resume does not boast a number of degrees nor certificates. I simply have a love for Jesus and the desire to share that love with as many people as I can.

So, let's spend some time together. I would like to tell you about my friend. His name is Jesus.

Love and peace to you,

Becky Hussey

Revelations

One evening, I sat upon my sofa with my dog, a black and white cocker spaniel named Pepper, nestled at my side. I was watching and listening to *Larry King Live* on CNN. His guests were analyzing a high profile murder case in which DNA played a large role. Dr. Henry Lee, a forensic expert, spoke of DNA and mitochondrial DNA. I enjoyed listening to Dr. Lee, partly because he is very interesting and partly because I use to live less than a mile from the University of New Haven where his School of Forensic Science is located. He and the other guest experts bantered back and forth about the various intricacies of the science as it related to the case. I found myself thinking about how God put us together so perfectly and how every minute detail was accomplished. Science was working on figuring it out; but, God created it.

Since then, I have found myself noticing and observing details in people and in nature that are so marvelous that it makes God's awesomeness even more awesome than I ever previously considered. One morning, I sat on the front porch with a hot cup of coffee, drinking in the coffee as well as the fresh morning air. I was reading the Bible, studying the words as part of my daily devotion. Again, my sweet cocker spaniel was at my feet. We both enjoyed the warmth of the sun cascading down upon us. I loved how the warmth of the sun felt on my skin and basked it in. I knew Pepper was enjoying it, too. She stretched out near me, her head touching my foot. She was content to be close by like this. Her desire to be close warmed my heart as much as the sun warmed my skin.

In between chapters, I would gaze out over the landscape. My neighbor's houses looked so homey that day. The mountain ridge in the distance appeared sharp and clear. No fog obscured my view. On a clear day, it is not unusual to hear the enchanting cadence of the high school marching band as they practice for an upcoming parade or football game.

The distant, yet distinct, sound provides hometown charm to any morning or evening. This particular day was no exception. The sound rose up to meet me and I welcomed it. Memories of my own high school's marching band fleeted through my mind. A small bird, perhaps a wren of some kind, landed on the porch rail in front of me. It was so close that I could have reached out to touch it if I had wanted. Pepper saw it, too. She raised her head to look at it. We both sat there and watched it as it watched us. I could see her tiny eyes looking at me and her head tilting from one side to the other. Here was this little creature, knit together by God's hand, made by the same Creator that made my dear little dog and the same Creator that made me.

Ah, and there it was again, the realization of how interconnected we really are. We all have God's DNA within us. We are all born into this world by the same Maker. As I turned my attention back to my study of God's Holy Word, I recalled the lessons that I have learned in my own life-lessons that were much like those taught in the Bible. I saw the patterns and knew that it was written for us to use in our lives. It was not intended to remain an ancient document, with a purpose applicable only to those who lived many centuries ago; but, rather, it is to be a living textbook for all generations. Today, God uses the events in our lives to mold and shape us into the people that He created us to be just as He did in the lives of Abraham, Isaac and Moses. We all have a purpose and a plan. I have heard preachers speak similar words and I have read wonderful books with similar thoughts projected; but, on this day, it was all so clear. The beauty of God's earth, the sweetness of the creatures that He brought to life, combined with the complexity of our own humanness is all a part of the universe. Each one is unique, different and separate in their being; yet, they contain the same particles. The difference is that they are wrought together differently. They are formed and structured differently. In the discovery of this reality, it is impossible to deny the awesome power of God.

A flower has purpose. Its purpose from the time it is a seedling is to grow and to bloom. The same is true for us only our blossoms look a little different. Our purpose is placed within our hearts. God equips us with what we need to accomplish our purpose. The truth of this is detailed over and over again throughout the Bible. There is no need for us to think that the same won't be done for us. It is learning to trust that truth that is hard. In my first book, *Refiner's Fire*, I shared about how I tried very hard to escape my purpose and often meddled in God's plans for me by not listening to the instructions or by becoming impatient. I am certain that most of you reading this book will say the same is true for yourselves as well.

I have come to understand that my purpose is to teach, not mathematics, nor science; but, to teach about Jesus, the Word of God, and the principles of leading a Christian life. When I was a child, I remember enjoying writing on a chalkboard and explaining things that I had learned. I have also always had a great love for reading and writing. I would write little stories and essays. So, when I was a teenager attending the Lutheran Church, I responded when our pastor said there was a need for substitute teachers and teacher's aides in the Sunday School program. It was not long until I had my own class and later on helped with the organizing and structuring of the classes. I taught a junior high class as well as second grade.

Throughout high school, I always enjoyed writing assignments the most. Because of this, I decided to begin writing for fun. I would write short stories and create characters; but, I never seemed to be able to finish the story. It was much later that I realized that I was not using the writing skills for the purpose that God had intended them to be used.

Once I graduated from Juniata High School in Mifflintown, Pennsylvania, and eventually moved to Connecticut, I found myself busy with my job and then later with my children. All the while, I wanted to write and kept finding myself back in positions where people were asking me to teach or to write for them in some capacity.

When my first child was born, I began attending a Catholic Church in Stratford, Connecticut. I remember speaking with Monsignor Pitoniak in his office one afternoon. My daughter, Carissa, was just a baby at the time. While the priest and I spoke, she lay comfortably under a blanket in her carrier. We talked about many things that day; but, I remember the priest asking me if I would like to get involved in the religious education program at Holy Name of Jesus. He said that, with my experience as a Sunday School teacher in the Lutheran Church, I would be an asset. He also pointed out that because I was familiar with Catholic teachings given my Catholic school education when I was a young child it would be an easy adjustment. Well, I thought about it; but, with having a new baby, I did not feel I could dedicate myself to this kind of work at the time. I explained my concern about that and he agreed; but, he suggested that I keep the thought on the back burner. I did. Little did I know, then, that later on, I would find myself not only teaching but directing a religious education program at a Catholic church in West Haven, Connecticut.

The truth is that I resisted the call to teach for some time and as I gave in to the call, I realized that there was more to it. Each of the steps that I had taken had prepared me for another part of the plan and I was being drawn closer and closer to doing what I was called to do. Now, it is clear that God wants me to use my love for writing to tell others about His son, Jesus, and to encourage people to trust His direction, to learn from the Word of God and to live our lives in accordance with these teachings. It is also very clear to me that God wants me to use my teaching ability to instruct adults, teens and children in group settings or one on one. For myself, I have found a whole new meaning to the saying "the whole world is a classroom". I had never thought of it this way before; but, teaching people about Christ can be done anywhere at anytime. It does not have to be in a structured religious education program or Sunday School Class. It can be done in the grocery store check out line!

Scripture tells us that God knows every intricate detail of each of us. He even knows how many hairs we have on our head. This is how close He is to us. If we can grasp hold of this thought, then we will know the depth of the love He has for us. He has not set us here on Earth to fail. He wants us to flourish and to thrive. Throughout the next several chapters, we will be exploring various scripture passages that reveal the truths about His love for us. In each case, I have provided stories from my own life, observations that I have made and revelations that have been opened up to me. Without the Word of God, I would only be scratching the surface of these truths. With the Word of God, I can see the truth, grow from it, and ultimately share it.

Luke 12:6-9

"Are not five sparrows sold for two small coins? Yet not one of them has escaped the notice of God. Even the hairs of your head have all been

counted. Do not be afraid. You are worth more than many sparrows. I tell you, everyone who acknowledges me before others the Son of Man will acknowledge before the angels of God. But whoever denies me before others will be denied before the angels of God."

Tiramisu
"Lift Me Up"

Tiramisu, a creamy, delectable Italian dessert, is one of my favorite treats. But, now, I cannot say the word without thinking of my former boss, the late Rev. Peter J. Pinto. The day before he died, Father Peter and I, along with the rectory housekeeper, Rosalia Nieves, had a conversation about tiramisu. Father Peter had a great love for languages; so, when Rosalia and I wondered what the Italian word meant, he tried to decipher it for us. He wrote the word on the chalkboard in the hallway at the rectory and tried to break it down for us. I remember him thinking aloud as he studied the word. He said something like this, "I think it has something to do with love." Rosalia and I had laughed and teased him. He was of Italian decent and surely knew very well that *amore* was the Italian word for love. He had laughed about it, too. We all thought about Father Anthony Licastro that day. He had died in the Spring after a battle with cancer. He, too, had a love for languages. Italian was his native language though he was fluent in English, French, Spanish and Latin. Had he been with us, he would not only have provided the meaning of the word; but, we likely would have gotten an hour long class on the Italian language. It would have been just fine with all of us because he was captivating when he taught. Not only could he capture your attention with his voice and words; but, his hand gestures and facial expressions would demonstrate the lesson as well. He could emphasize his points with his eyes and his hands better than anyone I knew.

We did not figure out the meaning of the word that day. Instead, we went back to the kitchen to have our coffee and our conversation moved on to other topics. I had been concerned about Father Peter that day. He seemed a little mixed up and had even asked me if the lights were flickering. I remember saying, "no Father, the lights are not flickering.

Let's go in the kitchen to relax. I'm going to make coffee." That's when we had the tiramisu conversation. I tried to tell myself that it was the pain medication. But, deep down I knew he was in his final hours. You see, Father Peter had bone cancer. He had dealt with prostate cancer in 1994 and had been cancer free all this time. Then, there it was, back again, in another form. Father Peter never really came out and told us what his prognosis was. But, somehow I knew the day that he told me about it that the prognosis was not a good one. I remember praying for him and encouraging others to pray for him. Yet, I sensed from deep within that he was going to be called home to the Lord. I remember distinctly having a conversation with the cook and the housekeeper in the month of June. Father Peter had told Patty and Rosalia about his illness; but, he had not elaborated on his condition. They had come to me to talk about it. I remember saying to them, that day, that he would be gone before Christmas. The words had come out of my mouth before I could stop them. It had been a word of knowledge from the Holy Spirit. I knew it. Both Patty and Rosalia resisted my words and did not want to think it possible. In the next couple of months, although he was more tired than usual, he seemed to be doing fairly well. I allowed myself to push the knowledge away.

The next day, he was dead. He never came down from his room that cool, late October day. He had died peacefully in his sleep. After working for him for eighteen years, I was overwhelmed with a variety of emotions: grief, relief that he didn't have to suffer a long and painful demise, and joy that he was going home to be with our Lord, Jesus. Father Chacko Kumplam, a friend of Father Peter and the chaplain of Saint Raphael Hospital in New Haven, had come over to the rectory right away upon learning the news. He made the calls to the Chancery of the Archdiocese of Hartford and I made the difficult call to Father Peter's family. I was able to get in touch with his sister-in-law who would then pass the word on to the nieces and nephews.

Parishioners began to hear the news and someone had to take charge. I stepped into the role; but, a part of me just wanted to take some time to grieve for my friend. It was a busy time, too, nearly overwhelming. There was so much to do. In addition to the normal daily functions I performed at the church, I had many phone calls to make, arrangements to discuss, and problems to solve. I had done a lot for Father Pinto as his condition had worsened; but, now, I was doing a lot more. It was a stressful time for us all. I spent a lot of time on the telephone with the Archbishop's office that week making sure that we did everything just right. I was never more happy to have my friend Judi and her husband Matt Finkle come to the rectory to be with me the day after Father Peter died. When my friend, Rose Majestic, called, I remember telling her that I needed my friends around me. She was a close friend of Father Peter, too. She came right away. Many of Father Peter's friends gathered. To me, Bill Kottage and his parents, William and Grace, were more like his family than friends. It was extremely comforting for all of us to be together during this difficult time.

It was the day after Father Peter died when Rosalia and I noticed the word, tiramisu, written on the chalkboard. The realization that it was the last word he had written before his death seemed to haunt us. Neither of us dared to erase the word for weeks. We wondered about it, reflected on the significance of it; yet, neither of us ever looked it up to see what it meant. It was as though we thought the word held some secret message that we were afraid to hear.

It was a year and a half later when I shared the story with my sisters, niece, nephew and his wife. My nephew immediately got on his lap-top and within moments, a click of the mouse here, a click of the mouse there, and boom, there it was: Tiramisu meant "lift me up" or "pick me up". While I realized, immediately, that the reference was in connection to the lift you get after enjoying a special treat (after all we are talking about a rich, Italian dessert here) I could not deny the prophetic aspect of the translation. A Catholic priest's final written word meant "lift me up". Could he have been saying to our Heavenly Father, "'lift me up' to heaven, I'm ready to go home"?

For several months after Father Peter died, I felt badly that I had not taken the time to tell him in those last hours how much I loved and appreciated him. Even though I had a strong sense that he was in his final hours, I did not want to acknowledge it, even blocked it from my thoughts. I felt guilty for not contacting his friend, Matt Bernardi, so that he could come spend some time with him that evening. I convinced myself that he would think I was some sort of alarmist. After all, Father Peter did not appear to be in any distress, had not called his doctor, nor complained in any way. He simply seemed a little confused.

Later, I would talk to Matt about my thoughts and feelings. He shared his last conversation with Father Peter, and I realized that he had spoken to him the evening before he died, and the conversation had left him unsettled, too. We both found comfort in knowing each other's feelings and emotions at the time.

Now, I realize that Rosalia and I had done exactly what we were supposed to do. Our final conversation with Father Peter took place at the kitchen table at the rectory over a cup of coffee. He was comfortable and at peace, sitting with people who loved him. Yes, we were his staff, his employees; but, we really were family in the truest sense of the word, a collective group of people, living (working) under the same roof, nurturing, supporting and loving one another while working together to share our love for Jesus with others through our work.

A lot of people had a misconception about my work at the rectory. They pictured a calm, quiet atmosphere with the priest quietly studying as he prepared his homilies or read his Bible. But, it was rarely quiet. The phone and the doorbell rang a lot. There were people with problems, weddings to plan, sick parishioners to visit, funerals to arrange, and baptisms to perform and confessions to hear. Father Peter not only had to deal with spiritual matters but practical matters, as well, such as taking care of the leak in the roof of the church or the plumbing problem in the school.

As the administrative assistant, I took care of the parish files, paid the bills, prepared the weekly bulletins and all parish correspondence. I wrote everything that Father Peter needed written whether it was a note to a parishioner or the prayer for the Mayor's inauguration. He rarely felt the need to change anything. We worked well together. There were times that we got exasperated with each other. At times, I thought he took an awfully hard attitude toward some people. I also went through a period of time when I thought he took advantage of my willingness to work and rarely showed any appreciation for it. But, even though I would get annoyed at something he would say or do, I would get angry if anyone else criticized him. Today, I know that Father Peter had been one of those people that God puts in our life to mold and to shape us into the people we are called to be. I also realized that he was like many others that God had called into service who stumbled and made mistakes. Looking back on it all, I realize, we really did act more like family than staff, complete with good times and bad, arguments as well as great, memorable conversations, too. After his death, I heard from several people that Father Peter had shared with them how much he appreciated my assistance. It made my heart glad to know that all those years of hard work and dedication had not gone unnoticed.

I have many fond memories of the years I spent at Saint Louis Church. From the beginning when Jean Polletta was the bookkeeper, Marguerite Etzel was the cook and Henry and Shirley Duda, were the custodian and housekeeper, respectively, to later on when it was Patty Bassetti that cooked, Rosalia did the housekeeping and Mauro Campelo served as the custodian, we were always working together for the church. We along with the deacons and music director and all the parishioners made up the parish family with Father Peter leading the flock.

Father Peter loved a fresh brewed pot of coffee. If he thought the pot had sat on the burner for any length of time, he would insist that we make a new pot. Marguerite and I use to laugh about it. Then later, Rosalia and I use to find it highly amusing when Father Peter would call one of us on the intercom and ask us to make "fresh" coffee. More often than not, we knew exactly what he was going to ask before we would answer the call. Rosalia would hear my phone buzz and would run down the hall from the kitchen to poke her head in my office as I was answering the phone. She would mouth the words *"fresh coffee"* as I was hearing Father Peter saying the words in my ear. It took all I had within myself not to laugh out loud. It became an inside joke for us and Father Peter was only too happy to play his part. He was well aware of how we were amused by his coffee call and was delighted to provide the amusement. Oh, how we miss those calls now.

It was during those years working at Saint Louis Church that I experienced the most spiritual growth. I came to understand the importance of being a part of a community of believers. Through a variety of means, I came to understand the importance of confession and repentance. I got to see up close how hard pastor's work and how critical and difficult the parishioners could be. All along, I'm sure the Lord was preparing me for what He was calling me to do. As noted earlier, the Lord had placed a passion for writing on my heart and the years of working with Father Peter at Saint Louis Church had given me many opportunities to do just that. You'll see later on some other plans the Lord had for me.

Father Peter imparted much wisdom to me. He was a spiritual father: sharing, instructing, leading, guiding, correcting, and loving. There were times when he seemed overwhelmed and vulnerable. There were times when I thought he made mistakes. Initially, I was troubled by the stumbles and missteps. It seemed to me that men and women in leadership positions should be operating from a level of understanding that took them beyond some of the struggles that the average person faces. But, I quickly learned that we are all still growing and learning. Christian maturity is an on-going project.

For most of us, it is in those moments of vulnerability and weakness that we realize how much we need God's guidance and direction. When I read the examples of the great spiritual fathers from the Old Testament, like Abraham and Moses, I saw that they made mistakes, too. Like them, we learn from our mistakes and grow as children of God. I realized, too, that sometimes we have to re-learn lessons. Because we are bombarded by worldly thinking and temptations daily, there are times when even the strongest people fail.

Now, when I look back on Father Peter's life as a priest, I can clearly see a man who loved the Lord and did his best to do the work that he was called to do. I find it quite remarkable that, even in his final written word, he was still teaching, still leading, still setting an example. After much prayer, I believe the word—tiramisu, was a two-fold message.

First, it was Father Peter's final prayer to His Heavenly Father, "lift me up", I'm ready to go home. Secondly, it was a word given to Father Peter from God to share with his staff, family and friends, lift Me up. It was God's call to remember to give glory to God and to God alone. Father Peter wrote down the word that was given to him from God, perhaps not even fully aware of the meaning himself. I think Father Peter was right after all. Tiramisu did have something to do with love—Love between our Heavenly Father and us and our love for our Creator, our Shepherd. Now, Father Peter's final word, a prophetic word, through this book can be shared with the world through me. I do not think it is a coincidence that tiramisu is one of my favorite desserts. Every time I enjoy this treat, it will serve as a reminder to lift up the name of the Lord every chance I get. It will also serve as a precious reminder of my friend, Father Peter.

Rescue me from my enemies, my God;
lift me out of reach of my foes.
Psalm 59:2

Hear my cry, O God,
listen to my prayer!
From the brink of Sheol I call;
my heart grows faint.
Raise me up, set me on a rock,
for you are my refuge,
a tower of strength against the foe.
Psalm 61:2-3

Ways to "Lift God Up"

1. Listen to and sing praise and worship songs.
2. Praise God in your prayers everyday.
3. Do not be afraid to witness to others about the things that the Lord is doing in your life.
4. Be obedient to God's commandments and directions.
5. Confess sins immediately and repent.

Sinking Sand

I would like to share with you a little bit about how I ended up back in Pennsylvania after living in Connecticut for twenty-five years to illustrate how God has been working in my life. It took me some time to see it and to understand it; but, once I began to recognize God's hand in my life, many things started to become sharper and clearer.

I graduated from Juniata High School in Mifflintown, Pennsylvania. I had been living in Port Royal with my mother and twin sister. Central Pennsylvania is a beautiful region with rolling hills, lush valleys and majestic mountain ridges. We had a great view of the Tuscarora Mountain Ridge from our home in Port Royal. The often muddy Juniata River and the many creeks and streams provide fishing and rafting fun for those who enjoy the water. As I look back on the several states in which I lived (Idaho, Maryland, Connecticut, Indiana, Tennessee and Pennsylvania), I have come to appreciate something special about each of them. The beauty of the land is one of the most prominent attractions of Pennsylvania. One of my favorite images from my teenage years in Port Royal is driving in to Port Royal over the steel bridge that spans the Juniata River. There is a rather sharp grade down as you come off the bridge and onto the main street in town. When I learned how to drive, I use to think it was quite fun to come sweeping over the bridge and rushing down that hill. Ironically, I had a similar image that stuck with me from when we lived in Bristol, Tennessee. We lived in the Forest Hills III subdivision of homes in Bristol. It was a neighborhood of new homes when we arrived there from our move from Indiana. We had to go over a big hill and down the other side to enter the housing development. I can distinctly recall my father driving his big silver Buick over the hill and down the other side. As much as the image, I recall the distinct sensation that it created. I realize now that the sensation I got coming off the Port

Royal Bridge was the same; but, what made it so special was the link to the past—a reminder of my father and a reminder of a place that I loved. Bristol had been my favorite home of all the places we had lived. Most probably, Bristol will always hold a special place in my heart because that's where my father died. My most recent and strongest memories of my father, and those of which I am most fond, took place there. It's special to me, too, because this is the place that established my interest in car racing. It was my friend, Judy Foran, who later died of leukemia, who introduced me to names like Richard Petty and Bobby Allison. From then on, I began to follow stock car racing. At first, I followed it just a little bit; then, as the years went by, my interest grew. I avidly followed the careers of Rusty Wallace and Dale Earnhardt and delight in watching both of their sons race now.

My first job was at the Port Royal Speedway, a ½ mile clay oval situated on the Juniata County Fair Grounds. I worked in the concession stands and delighted in the race track atmosphere. At the time when I was working, Jimmy Spencer, who later went on to NASCAR fame, was racing there. I can still hear his name called out over the loud speaker. A few years later, it always made me smile when I would see him on television participating in NASCAR events. It was, yet another, pleasant link to the past that made my heart glad. I believe that God creates these special links for us to enjoy if we only take the time to notice them. Sometimes, we get so caught up in getting through our days that we forget to enjoy some of these simple treats.

After graduation, I applied for and was offered an office job at KB-Aerotech in the Lewistown, Pennsylvania Industrial Park. I worked in the order billing department. It was enjoyable work. I enjoyed taking telephone orders for the ultrasonic products that our company manufactured and I never minded doing data entry work. I had the added bonus of working with a nice group of people. (Ironically, now, many years later the mother of my first on-the-job supervisor and my mother are in the same room at the William Penn Nursing Facility in Lewistown, PA.) Less than two years later, I saw a job opportunity at corporate headquarters in Connecticut and took it. I became the lead word processing operator. I wish I could say that my intentions were great, noble intentions. They were not. My sole purpose was to break free from what I perceived as an ultra conservative life and find a man that would love me. Somehow, I didn't feel like that would happen in Pennsylvania. The men that visited from corporate headquarters in Connecticut were handsome, sophisticated men. Somehow, in my young and rather naïve mind, I thought that my chances of finding a wonderful husband would be greater in Connecticut. My mind returned to when I lived in Connecticut as a child. I remember my father going to the train station to head into New York for his engineering job with Westinghouse. His office was in the PanAm Building. Getting on a train to go into New York and then returning home to our beautiful home, in a nice neighborhood in Riverside, Connecticut, a town adjacent to Greenwich and Cos Cob, seemed like a grand adventure to me.

But, a child's perspective is much different than an adult. Yes, there were certainly many great things about living in Connecticut: the close proximity to Long Island Sound, the beautiful art galleries, interesting museums, and yet near enough to country living that within a short drive one could find an apple orchard or pumpkin patch to enjoy. But, I quickly found out that living in Connecticut is quite different than living in rural Central Pennsylvania. The pace is a lot faster. Traffic is brutal. People tend to be a lot more suspicious and aggressive. It took awhile to get used to it. There was something exciting about it; yet, I missed the more tranquil, serene life I knew back in Pennsylvania. From the moment I moved to Connecticut, my life was full of ups and downs. Though my mother and my sister and I had regularly attended church during my teen years, once I moved, I rarely attended church. My prayer life was weak and I don't remember spending any time reading the Bible during that time. I had allowed things of the world to influence my life. I also had gotten away from teaching. I had been teaching Sunday School at the Lutheran Church in Port Royal, Pennsylvania, and was getting more and more involved in various church activities. This is very important to note as I would repeat this same behavior later on and get myself into even more trouble.

Not very long after my move, I met a man. He was the "bad boy" type you read about in magazines, the complete opposite of myself. He was into Harley's and beer. Despite the differences, we started dating right away. I believe, now, that in my desire to have a loving relationship, I chose to ignore some things that were obvious. Much quicker than I should have, I got married and we soon had our first child. It was then that I regained my senses. The reality of having to be responsible for another life must have awakened my sense of responsibility and self. I started to attend church regularly again, only this time, it was a Catholic Church, and within a short time converted to Catholicism. It was not a big change for me. My sister Bobby and I had attended Catholic elementary schools; so, I was already familiar with much of the doctrine and the Mass was not much different from the order of service at the Lutheran Church that we attended as teenagers. Sure, there were some differences; but, not overwhelming differences.

I started to work on repairing my relationship with God by building up my prayer life. Soon, I had two children and found myself struggling with being married to an alcoholic. By the time my daughter was six and my son was three years old, I was working at the church. While I wanted my marriage to work, I felt that there was no way to repair it. Even though I had mixed emotions about it, I came to the conclusion that a divorce was the only solution. That's just what I did. I got divorced. My son got into some trouble. I had car problems, financial problems and health problems. My son got into even more trouble. I ended up working three jobs to try to make ends meet. My house burned down. I could go on and on. But, I think you get the picture. Things were just not going well and nothing ever seemed quite right. In fact, it seemed like my life was unraveling as fast as I could knit it back together.

A Proverb comes to mind when I look back at those times in my life. Proverbs 14:12 says this: "Sometimes a way seems right to a man but the end of it leads to death." It was quite evident that some of my choices were not prudent choices. Some were even sinful choices. As I worked through the stress of all these situations, I began to realize that God had been speaking to me throughout it all. Numerous times, I know I heard His voice giving me direction; but, quite often, I would allow my own thinking to override what I know I heard. I would become impatient and wanted things to happen right away. I failed to see that God's timing was perfect and mine was always a bit off. My decisions were not grounded in Godly wisdom; but, rather human reason. Once I started to realize that my choices were really disobedience toward God, I knew I had to repent and begin to listen. My stubbornness and eagerness to have quick results undermined the path that God was preparing for me. Instead of stable, solid ground, I was on constantly shifting ground. As a result, I stumbled and fell often. I repented of my disobedience and started to listen. Immediately, I began to see the world in a different light. It took quite a bit of time to dig myself out of the hole that I had dug for myself through my disobedient choices and impatience. But, God offered me a hand and pulled me up out of the hole. As I write these words of testimony, I can offer nothing but thanks and praise to the Creator of the Universe, God our Father, and His Son, Jesus Christ, our Lord and Savior.

This very crucial point was illustrated to me one day in a very, vivid way. I lived in the shoreline town of West Haven, Connecticut, and used to walk regularly on the beach. One afternoon after work, I was walking along in the sand, enjoying God's beautiful creation. There was no one around. I did not see a single person that evening as I walked. The sun was beginning to dip down below the tree line and the colors of the sunset cast a beautiful array of pinks, reds, purples and blues across the sky which then reflected on the rippling waters of Long Island Sound. It was truly a beautiful scene and a tranquil back drop for the end of a busy day.

Then, suddenly, I found myself plunging into a sink hole! I have heard people use the expression of your life flashing before your eyes at the onset of a catastrophic event; but, I had never had it happen to me. My life literally flashed before my eyes. It happened so fast that, before I knew it, I was thigh deep in wet sand and still sinking. I cried out loud to God and at that very moment I realized that if I threw myself forward and to the right just a little bit, I might be able to grab a hold of some rocks that were jutting out of the sand near me. I managed to lurch myself forward just enough to reach them and pulled myself out of the hole. It was not easy. My jeans were wet and made my legs feel like an anchor in the sand. The sand was so soft and loose that I had nothing to push my feet on to give me leverage. But, I got a hold of the rock and pulled myself forward. With some effort, I used both hands to hoist myself up. With the rock to hold on to, I managed to crawl out of that sink hole. I remember looking down at myself. My clothes were wet and full of sand; but, I was safe. I was shaking from head to toe; but, I was fine. My fear turned into gratitude. As I walked back to my car, I felt a sense of peace and security. The trembling began to subside and I did not even mind my wet clothes any more. Once to my car, I looked back at the water lapping up onto the sand. As I looked around, there were still no people. Occasionally, a car went by; but, it was evident from here in the parking lot that I would not have been seen from the roadway. Had it not been for that rock, I may not have been able to pull myself out of the hole. The tide would have come in and well, it could have been a terrible outcome. So, now, every time I sing the words of a favorite hymn, "On solid rock I stand, all other ground is sinking sand," I have a firm understanding of what those words mean. Without Jesus to grab on to, we cannot survive the pit falls in life!

As I pondered this major life lesson, I was drawn to one of Jesus' teachings.

Everyone who comes to me and hears my words and does them,
I will show you what he is like.
He is like a man building a house, who dug deep
and laid the foundation on the rock.
And when the flood came, the stream broke against the house and
could not shake it, because it had been well built But the one who
hears and does not do them is like a man who built his house on the
ground without a foundation. When the stream broke against it, imme-
diately it fell and the ruin of that house was great.
Luke 6:47-49 (ESV)

After reflecting on this passage, I realized that God was speaking to me quite clearly. I needed to have my foundation built upon rock. I could no longer continue to use human reason and worldly logic to face every day life. Jesus is my rock. Without His holy example, without His direction, without His Holy Word, without His *sacrifice,* I have nothing on which to stand. When I think back over the times when I was disobedient to God's direction, I shudder. (Be sure to read the chapter later on in this book about building blocks. I will build on this idea using other scriptures to reinforce the ideas brought out here.)

I have also seen how Satan tries to get us off the path. He uses deception to pull us into his web of lies. When our attention is off of God's Word, we are weak and vulnerable. Satan makes his path look good and wonderful. He plants an idea in our minds that we need to work out things ourselves. He's the one that tricks us into thinking that God is taking too long to answer our prayers. It's at that point that we try to rush ahead and fix things our way. Only, when we do that, there is usually a consequence to our foolishness.

It was only a matter of moments after I pulled myself out of the sink hole, by the grace of God, when I began to ask God if there was a lesson in this for me. I was sitting in my car, in my wet jeans, when I heard His response. *Remember what you were thinking about at the time.* I did remember and I was embarrassed. I had begun to revisit some angry thoughts I had about my relationship with my ex-husband. I had said that I had forgiven him for any hurt that he had caused me and hoped that he had forgiven me for any pain I caused him; yet, I was feeling bitter about being alone and feeling like I had been done some major disservice. My resentment had opened the door for Satan to come rushing in to remind me of all the things that were wrong with my life—I was alone. I was working three jobs to make ends meet. I didn't feel appreciated. I didn't feel loved or even needed by anyone. Then, I dropped into the sink hole. It was all too clear that I had become so absorbed in my poor me song that I had failed to watch where I was stepping, failed to take into consideration that the tide had gone out and some undermining had occurred. If I had been paying attention, I would have realized that the sand had gotten quite soft where I was walking. I could have simply moved a little bit closer to the drier sand. But, no, I was absorbed in my sorrow for myself and the consequence was that I stepped into a sink hole. Then, the message was clear. Satan's path leads to destruction. Jesus' path leads to salvation. I called out to Jesus, my rock, and He saved me. I repented of my ugly thoughts right then and there.

So, with that said, despite some of my stupidity and entirely because God was leading me through some of the lessons that I learned through my struggles, I have come to realize that God has equipped us all with certain gifts that we are to use on our life's journey. In addition to the gifts of the Holy Spirit that are available to use when we receive the Baptism of the Holy Spirit, we are given talents that we are to use to fulfill our purpose in life. All my life, I have loved to write. While some of my classmates in school dreaded writing essays for homework, I loved it. As I mentioned earlier, in Connecticut, I worked for eighteen years at a Catholic church. The pastor allowed me to take the reigns of all the writing for the parish. So, over the years, I used the gift of writing that God had given to me and I did it happily; but, I've always had a desire to write and to have my work published. With that goal in mind, I wrote several short stories and in the last couple of years started to work on writing a novel. Not only did I find the writing to be therapeutic during stressful times; but, I also felt like I was working toward my goal to someday have my work published. But, with working three jobs and struggling through trial after trial, I was not making much progress. You see, the timing was not right yet. I needed to trust in God's timing, not my own.

Then, after my house in Connecticut burned and was eventually rebuilt, I decided to put the house on the market and sell it. I had been thinking about moving back to Pennsylvania to be closer to my mother and sister. My mother had suffered through a rough Winter that year and had to be hospitalized a couple of times. I began to feel a need to spend more time with her instead of being limited to four or five trips from Connecticut a year. I prayed about it and I felt that God was telling me that I should go forward with my plans. So, when the house sold in two days, I knew I was on the right track. I found a house in Lewistown, Pennsylvania, and within 45 days I was all moved in. Since I did not have a job lined up yet, I realized that I could spend my time writing while I was looking for a job. God, the Master Creator, had worked out an opportunity for me to do some writing. The first draft of my novel was finished. It was time for a thorough edit to fix up some of the holes in the plot and polish the wording. Now, I had the time I needed to do it; yet, curiously, I found myself struggling with it for a few days and just could not seem to get going on it. During those days, several times during prayer, I felt the Lord was telling me to work instead on the inspirational book that I had been thinking about writing. I felt that He was prompting me to put the novel aside for the time being and work on sharing some of the lessons that I learned. Having already learned my lesson in obedience the hard way, I knew I had to listen. The words to Isaiah 30:31 rang in my ears. "While from behind a voice shall sound in your ears: "This is the way: walk in it," when you would turn to the right or to the left." God was telling me exactly what to do and He was giving me the time to do it. I set to work right away. From May on, I wrote every morning until it was finished. My job search had not yielded anything; but, I continued to write, visit my mother, attend job fairs and enjoy getting reacquainted with the area. After the stressful year I had endured the year before with the fire and some of the other difficulties I had experienced, I found myself feeling rested, refreshed and at peace. I realized that the peace that I was feeling had come because I was doing what God wanted me to do. In the New Testament book of Philippians, Chapter Four verse 7, Paul writes "the peace of God that surpasses all understanding will guard your hearts and minds in Christ Jesus." For the first time in my life, I felt this peace and relished it. I was fulfilling a purpose: God's purpose.

It was quite evident to me that God had been dealing with me for a long time. Leading me back to Pennsylvania, I believe, was God's way of physically taking me back to where I originally got off track. While I can clearly see now when and where I went wrong, I can also see that everything I experienced during the time I was in Connecticut, has provided spiritual training and preparation for what God has been calling me to do for some time

When I finished the manuscript for the inspirational book in August, two days later I got a job with CVS Pharmacy. It was not exactly the kind of job that I had thought I would find; but, it was a job with benefits none the less. In the meantime, I started sending out query letters to various publishers.

Then, one day, I was talking to one of my co-workers at CVS. She shared with me that her fiancé, who also works with us, was having his book published. Naturally, my ears perked up immediately. I asked who the publisher was. She was delighted to tell me all about it. At that very moment, I could feel a tingle run up and down my spine. That evening, I went home and checked out the publisher's web-site. After reading the guidelines on sending manuscripts for consideration, I decided to send a query letter to the editor. In about two weeks, I got a letter inviting me to send in the manuscript for consideration. Just a little over two weeks later, I got another letter stating that the manuscript was being accepted for publication. I realized, then, that God, in His infinite wisdom, had placed me in a position where I would glean information that would enable me to reach my goal to be published. Each step of the way, God was at work.

Had I chosen to be disobedient, I could have missed an opportunity to realize a life long dream. I could have stubbornly chosen to continue to work on the novel despite the fact that I felt in my heart that God was telling me to work on a different project. I could have skipped applying for jobs at retail establishments because I had always done administrative work. But, I trusted the promptings of the Holy Spirit to go ahead and put my application in at CVS and K-Mart. I was actually offered a position at both places on the same day and chose CVS because they offered health benefits. Again, God steered and directed me in practical ways.

In sharing this testimony, I can serve as a witness to how God can work miracles in our lives on a daily basis if we only take the time to listen for his directions and then obey. Walking in obedience, I fulfilled a life long dream to have my work published. My first book entitled **Refiner's Fire** was published in April of 2006. I had achieved my goal while at the same time honoring and glorifying God. Alleluia!

> *Save me, God,*
> *For the waters have reached my neck.*
> *I have sunk into the mire of the deep,*
> *where there is no foothold.*
> *I have gone down to the watery depths;*
> *the flood overwhelms me.*
> **Psalm 69:2-3**

> *Rescue me from the mire;*
> *do not let me sink.*
> **Psalm 69:14**

Ways to Build a Firm Foundation Instead of on Sinking Sand

1. Read the Bible daily
2. Pray often, more than once a day.
3. Follow God's commandments and directions.

Spiritual Fathers and Mothers

In the previous chapter, I referred to my boss, Father Peter, as a spiritual father. A spiritual father is one who is not necessarily a father by blood; but, one who imparts spiritual direction and leadership into a person's life. I never really gave this concept much thought until I began attending a leadership class at my church. The lessons brought forth in the class caused me to think about the influence that our spiritual forefathers can have in our lives. After studying some of the teachings in the Old Testament, and as a follower of Jesus Christ, I believe I can see that we are, indeed, related to Abraham spiritually in that we have accepted the revelation that was prophesied through Abraham's faith when he was asked to sacrifice his son, Isaac. God asked Abraham to offer his son, Isaac, as a sacrifice. When Abraham obeyed by bringing his son to the mountain top and going as far as binding his son for the sacrifice, God did not expect him to carry out the sacrifice; but, instead provided the Ram for the sacrifice. These words in Holy Scripture offered a hint of what was to come as God offered his only Son in sacrifice for our sins. God made the sacrifice that He did not demand that Abraham make.

We can all relate and identify with Abraham as he developed his relationship with God. I have found myself in situations, like Abraham, when I tried to run ahead of God's plan and attempted to get results on my own without waiting for God's perfect timing to unfold. Just like Abraham stumbled when he identified Sarah as his sister and got into hot water in Egypt and again when he rushed ahead, at Sarah's prompting, to have a child with Hagar, I, too, have tried to make things happen on my own and regretted not waiting for God to work out the details for me. Read my first book *Refiner's Fire* and you'll see some of the things that I did. It is through these faltering steps that we learn to trust God's instruction and to train ourselves to hear his voice and to follow it. It is because

Abraham had come to know and trust God and to believe in His promises that he was able to take Isaac to the mountain that day and know to say to his son that God would provide the sacrifice.

As our faith life strengthens and matures, we, too, will be able to respond in confidence and follow God's every command without hesitation because we will know God's voice. We know from Abraham, our forefather, our spiritual father, that God always keeps His end of the covenant.

The spiritual inheritance that a believer receives as a result of our relationship to Abraham is an inheritance of faith. Through his example of faith, we see how a true, authentic relationship with God works. We see that there is real communication. We see that God not only hears us but also speaks to us. Galatians, Chapter 3, verse 6, says. "Thus Abraham believed God, and it was credited to him as righteousness." In following Abraham's example, we can lead righteous lives, as well, by hearing God, obeying His instructions, and believing God's promises.

In addition to the spiritual mothers and fathers that we can read about in the Bible, we also have spiritual mothers and fathers that are in our lives today to impart wisdom to us. My first spiritual mother and father were my parents who laid a moral foundation in my life. Father Peter was a spiritual father during a time when I needed to reconnect with God after a time of rebellion. Just working with him on a daily basis became a classroom where I could re-learn some basic truths that I had failed to use in my life. As I grew stronger, I was introduced to stronger people who could take me to another level of spirituality. Sister Anna Maria Hartmann, became a spiritual mother, imparting her wisdom. As a Maryknoll Sister, she had the opportunity to serve as a missionary in places like Nepal and Guatemala. For a time while back in the United States, she lived in the convent building on the property of Saint Louis Church where I worked. She worked closely with the large Hispanic population there. Her wisdom, strength and compassion for the people opened my eyes. Her example, woven together with the lessons that I had been given through others, helped me to grow more as a person and as a child of God. All the while, through these fine examples, I saw the necessity of immersing myself in the Holy Word of God and being sure to maintain open communication with God through prayer, not just me reciting a list of needs. I began to realize, more and more, that I was not allowing enough time to listen for God's response, for God's instructions during prayer. I was too busy talking about what I wanted. Now, I realize that we must remember to praise God, to lift Him up, always. We must confess our sins and repent of them. We must thank God for all He has done in our lives. It is through Him that we have life and all that is good. God already knows what we need and already knows the desires of our hearts. When we pray, we must remember to allow time to sit back and to listen for His instructions, His thoughts, and His response. These may come as a feeling in our heart, a feeling of peace and tranquility. It could come in the form of a picture in our mind or sometimes, even an audible voice. Yes, God does respond, always. When we don't hear His response, it's usually because we are not listening or do not like what He is saying.

After coming to respect the influence of spiritual mothers and fathers in my own life, as well as those in the Bible, I have a greater concern for how I may be influencing the lives of my children, my family, my friends and those whom I encounter each day. I can see the influence I have had in my daughter's life. Carissa has become an independent woman who is willing to work hard and to study well. She has the same compassion and love for animals that I do. She is pouring herself into her work at Bridgeport Hospital and her studies to become a nurse. I have also seen the influence I have had in my son's life. Timothy, despite the struggles that he encountered for a time, has developed into a hard-working young man.

When he called me to tell me that he had applied and been accepted to the College of Aeronautics, Timothy said that "he had taken a step up". He used a phrase that I can remember the exact moment when the wisdom behind it had been imparted.

Timothy knew that I enjoyed watching Joel Osteen's program on Sunday evenings. For those of you who are not familiar with Joel Osteen, he is the Pastor of Lakewood Church in Texas and his services are televised. There were a number of occasions when Tim would sit down with me to hear the sermon. On one of those evenings, Joel Osteen shared a great story which I have since found myself using to make a point either with my own children or those whom I taught in the religious education program I directed.

The story went something like this: One day a donkey fell down into the shaft of an old well. The farmer was upset not only because he needed the donkey to work in the fields but because he had a love for the animal as well. Well, the farmer could not get a rope down to pull him out because he feared he would hurt the animal in the effort. Unable to bear the sound of the donkey's pitiful cries, the farmer decided that the only thing to do would be to fill the well with dirt thus burying the animal and putting him out of his misery. Well, the donkey felt the dirt hitting his back; but, he did a remarkable thing. Instead of just standing there and allowing the farmer to bury him, as the dirt hit his back, he shook the dirt off and stepped up. He shook the dirt off and stepped up. He repeated this over and over again until he found he had risen to the top of the well. The farmer was amazed as he watched his donkey step up and out of the well! I loved the lesson so much that I told my students in the religious education program the story and often used the phrase "taking a step up" when referring to walking away from old, bad habits and adopting new, Christ-like behaviors.

This story illustrated how very important it is to demonstrate wisdom in all areas of our lives. We must always watch our words and our actions, even the television programs that we select. When we hear young children use foul language, it is not because these children just decided to start speaking this way. It is because they have been influenced by others to speak in this manner. We must be careful that our actions serve to uplift and bring about peace and love. At the same time, we must guard against behaviors that tear down and destroy with hatred, confusion and spite.

Just recall the last time you were in the company of a cranky, hate-filled person. Being in the presence of someone who is angry and bitter can bring a person down. This is why it is so very important to be grounded by prayer, have the power of the Word of God in your heart and mind and the indwelling of the Holy Spirit to protect you in these circumstances. Instead of being dragged into the mire yourself, you can infuse light and love into the heart of a troubled individual by speaking words of love and truth in Jesus' name.

"Paul, an apostle of Christ Jesus by command of God our savior and of Christ Jesus our hope, to Timothy, my true child in faith: grace, mercy and peace from God the Father and Christ Jesus our Lord." **1 Timothy 1:1-2**

Paul addresses Timothy as his true child of faith. He is Timothy's spiritual father, not his father by blood. He is guiding and instructing him in these New Testament letters. These letters are great examples of how one can impact the life of another in a positive way.

Finding a Spiritual Mother or Father

1. Attend church and bible study regularly to strengthen your faith and build up your knowledge of the Bible as well as enable you to be in contact with other Christians.
2. Select friends wisely.
3. Do not be afraid to make friends with older, more established Christians.
4. Do not avoid talking to the pastors, elders or others in leadership positions because you think they don't have time for you or worse yet because you think they will ask you to do something.

Being a Spiritual Mother or Father

1. Make wise choices.
2. Study the Word of God daily.
3. Pray daily.
4. Write letters of encouragement to children and to young people in your family and be sure to include scripture teaching or spiritual insights.
5. Attend church and bible study regularly to continue to increase your faith and your knowledge of the Bible.

Anger

For much of my life, I dealt with anger by suppressing it. For a number of years, if something made me angry, I simply chose not to deal with it. While I never resorted to using the silent treatment on those whom made me angry, what I did, instead, was to "swallow" the anger. This method of dealing with anger never resolved anything; but, quite frequently resulted in overeating, a method of "stuffing" my anger away. It also frequently resulted in bad headaches.

As I matured and began developing a relationship with Christ, the Lord showed me that I often used the expression "blew a gasket" when referring to being upset or irritated about a situation that made me angry. In thinking about that, I realized that this expression was so very accurate—pressure builds up inside and, at some point, something has to give in order to release the built up steam. This became abundantly clear to me after my Buick Skyhawk blew a head gasket. Then, my next car, a Thunderbird, blew a head gasket—twice. I vowed never to use the expression again; but, I also, realized that I needed a better way to deal with anger. Consequently, I am no longer building up pressure inside and there are no more blown head gaskets. In other words, I don't suffer from anywhere near as many headaches as I once did because I do not allow things to build up inside.

The Pastor at Grace Covenant Church in Lewistown, Ron Neff, taught a class on the book of Genesis. In one of our studies on a Wednesday evening, in discussing anger, Pastor Ron quoted Thomas A. Kempis, who said, "Be not angry that you cannot make others as you wish them to be, since you cannot make yourself as you wish to be." The Lord began to show me that some of the very things that I found upsetting and irritating in other people were things that I needed to work on myself. The root of the anger was actually within myself. The triggers would be bluntly worded criticisms or rejection. Now, I have realized that it is far better to follow the advice from Ephesians 4:36 and not let the sun go down on my anger. I have come to understand that it is far better to try to sit down and talk things through than to ignore the anger or to avoid dealing with it. Doing so brings about healing and understanding for all involved.

I think back to my failed marriage. In my first book, I stated that I would have handled things differently had I had a more mature relationship with the Lord. I would like to expand on that thought here. There were several problems within our marriage. I still love my ex-husband very much, so I am not going to denigrate him in these pages. Our failed marriage was as much my fault as his. While there was a time that I would have liked to have cited his alcohol problem as the lone factor in the demise of our marriage, I cannot honestly say that is true. The Lord has dealt with me on this issue and this is what I have learned. Our single largest problem was that God was not at the center of our marriage. While we were both Christians and I attended church regularly, even worked at the church, our home-life did not have Christ in the seat of honor. We did not pray together as a couple. Sure, I prayed and I am sure he did, too. We taught our children to pray. But, while I may have a word of prayer with the children from time to time, Ed and I did not pray together as a couple. We did not spend time reading the Word of God together either. When problems arose, we did not sit down and pray about it nor did we open our Bibles to consult the Word of God.

When our marriage began to unravel, a lot of people were shocked. Because I am not one to openly discuss my problems, I did not discuss our problems with a lot of people. There were only a handful of people who had any idea that there was something wrong. I did not want anyone to think I had failed as a wife or could not manage my family. Instead of seeking appropriate counsel, I kept my anger about the drinking to myself until I "blew a gasket". When we did seek help, we went to a counselor who did not really give us any tools to use to work things out. He spoke about divorce as though it were the only solution to the problem. If I had a chance to do this over, I would have insisted that we talk to a pastor who could give us guidance. I remember very well that after I filed for divorce, Ed called the priest for whom I worked and wanted him to try to change my mind. Father Peter was reluctant to get involved because I worked for him. My immediate belief was that all Ed wanted to do was to have someone persuade me not to go through with the divorce. I doubted that he wanted to make any changes in his own behavior.

If I had the maturity that I have developed since then, I would have agreed to pastoral counseling. It was not right for me to make the assumption that Ed did not want to make any changes within himself nor was it right for me to assume that he alone was the source of our problems. Instead, I stewed and steamed over past hurts, spewed all kinds of angry accusations, and refused to participate in any kind of talks. It was "tough love", I thought. I had been influenced by the secular world and modern psychology instead of depending on direction from God during a difficult time. All the while, I thought Ed would be so shaken that I had taken such dramatic steps that he would repent of his drinking and want to make things right. I was absolutely certain that he would never allow our relationship to come to an end and break-up our family. I was wrong. Instead of bringing about reconciliation, I further alienated him. Not only did it bring about more pain and more anger; but, now Ed did not trust me. Later, when we attempted to reconcile, the reconciliation failed because he could not get it out of his mind that I had left him once and might do it a second time.

I certainly do not want to imply that women have to tolerate abuse and to pretend that alcoholism is an acceptable term in a marriage. It is not. Both issues must be addressed. What I am saying is that we should have had God at the helm in our marriage. I firmly believe that we would be together to this day had we allowed Him to be in control of our lives.

While I cannot go back and change things, I can offer unconditional love and forgiveness toward my ex-husband now. I also have learned to forgive myself for my failure to handle things well. When I see young couples getting involved in serious relationships, I long to be able to impart some of the wisdom that I have learned over the years to help them avoid problems.

Recently, I had a conversation with my son about this very topic. He has met a beautiful young woman, Angela, whom he hopes to one day marry. As soon as he shared with me that they were thinking of a future together, I told him to start praying together as a couple and start reading the Word of God together. It is so very important to start things off right.

She agreed. I'm so looking forward to having this young lady as my daughter-in-law!

As parents, it is important that we impart wisdom to our children in plain terms. All too often, we hold back and don't want to interfere. But, sometimes, we need to open our mouths and speak the truth. My son was not offended that I offered advice in his relationship and neither was his girl friend. They accepted it because they know I love them.

In addition to the establishment of a solid prayer life and remembering to incorporate the wisdoms and truths found in the Bible in your daily reading, I believe that learning how to express feelings, disappointments and anger in a constructive, useful way from the beginning is the best way to start a relationship. When things do go wrong, it is imperative that wise counsel is sought immediately. A trusted pastor can be the key to preventing the destruction of a marriage. I am not saying that counselors and psychologists are not equipped to help; but, all too often, the spiritual connection, the Godly wisdom, is left out and worldly thinking reigns supreme.

"You have heard that it was said to your ancestors, 'You shall not kill; and whoever kills will be liable to judgment.' But I say to you, whoever is angry with his brother will be liable to judgment..." **Matthew 5:21-22**

How to Avoid Letting Anger Rule You

1. Daily prayer and Bible Study is imperative; but, one must also vow to never let your anger lead you to sin. This includes avoiding foul language and cursing when angry. This is sinful and pollutes the atmosphere with a negativity that fouls the opportunity for peace.
2. Teach your children from a young age how to deal with hurt feelings and anger; so, that bad habits are not nurtured through the teen years and brought into future relationships.
3. Parents should never allow a child to threaten, punch, bite, kick or attack others in anyway to resolve issues.

Teaching the Way Christ Taught

Jesus taught his disciples and the crowds that gathered around him by words and by actions. He provided a loving example in the way he met people in their needs. He healed people of their illnesses, forgave them of their sins, took pity on those who were in mourning and even restored life to some who had died. Jesus also used parables to make his points and, in doing so, made the lessons He taught easy to remember and to repeat. He also took advantage of meal times to gather people around him. I would imagine that they did not sit silently while they ate their meals. I suspect that they shared and discussed many things. Jesus, no doubt, used those meal times to teach His disciples and allow them an opportunity to ask questions and to talk.

I believe that we can utilize Christ's methods today by letting go of the idea that it is up to the pastors and elders of the church to minister and to reach out to people. All of us can begin to teach others by being sure that we are following the principles and teachings of Christ. It is then that we can reach out to those around us who are hurting and in need. When we offer a word of consolation to someone who is grieving, we open a door of opportunity to minister to that person. Offering to take someone to the doctor when she is sick or sharing a ride to work with someone whose car won't start allows the person in need to realize that someone cares. In John 14:34, Jesus said, "I give you a new commandment: love one another. As I have loved you, so you also should love one another. This is how all will know that you are my disciples, if you have love for one another". These situations provide us with a unique opportunity for us to share our personal stories of committing our lives to Christ. It is much easier for a person to accept a story of conversion when they can clearly see that the person who shared it is actually living a life modeled after Jesus by reaching out in love in a time of need.

I love how Paul wrote letters to the young church in Corinth, Ephesus and Thessalonica and how he wrote to young Timothy. These words of instruction and encouragement provided greatly needed guidance as well as morale boosters for new Christians. I have always enjoyed writing and I believe that God has called me to use this gift as a way to reach out and to minister to others. Whether it is a spiritual book that shares how God has influenced my life or a letter to a nephew who is still learning what it means to be a Christian, I believe that God wants me to use the written word as a means to reach out. Recently, one of my former Confirmation students wrote me a note. I, once again, felt that it was an opportunity to do more than just respond with the latest news. It was an opportunity to share my faith and encourage her as she deepens her relationship with Jesus.

I believe it is extraordinarily important for families to gather together at the kitchen or dining room table to share meals. Taking the time to eat together provides a perfect setting to teach, to instruct and to impart wisdom to your children. It seems today that our children's lives are filled with endless sports practices, dance classes and activities that take them away from home that it is nearly impossible to sit down together to enjoy the evening meal. Fast food restaurants and the ability to grab a frozen food to pop in the microwave have replaced home cooked meals. While it is certainly convenient, it deprives us of valuable family time.

When we sit together face to face at the dinner table, we can talk and share. When good things happen, we can celebrate it together. When bad things happen, we can work out a solution together or offer appropriate words of sympathy. When this opportunity to be together is eliminated, all too often it leads to young children shouldering burdens alone and/or figuring out a solution on their own without the benefit of the wisdom of someone older and more experienced. It is an opportunity for parents to see what their children are facing day to day as well to see them in person for an extended period of time. All too often, we miss things in our children's lives when we let them dart upstairs to their bedrooms with a quick hello and a hug. Then, when we discover that they are struggling with a drug or alcohol problem, it's a shock. I found myself looking back with regret at the time lost with my children. If I had insisted on eating meals together every day, I may have been more aware of what was going on in my son's life.

I have quite a few great memories of playing cards with my daughter and a couple of her girlfriends. We would talk and laugh while we played.

Sometimes we would talk so much that we would forget whose turn it was; but, still, we had so much fun. It was so nice to be able to share a cup of tea and simply enjoy each other's company. I felt blessed that Carissa and the girls wanted to spend time with me and honored that they felt comfortable to talk and to share things with me. But, most importantly, it was a chance for me to be an influence in their lives and to love them.

I can recall an evening when I had ten young people in my home, a combination of my daughter and her friends and my son and his friends and myself. Everyone ended up in my small dining room. We discussed everything from Dunkin' Donuts coffee to the consequences of sinful choices. No one felt threatened or judged. It was simply an opportunity for me to sow positive seeds into their lives. These young people, in turn, shared their thoughts and feelings with me and gave me a look into their world from their perspective.

As Jesus passed on from there, he saw a man named Matthew sitting at the customs post. He said to him, "Follow me." And he got up and followed him. While he was at table in his house, many tax collectors and sinners came and sat with Jesus and his disciples. The Pharisees saw this and said to his disciples, "Why does your teacher eat with tax collectors and sinners?" He heard this and said, "Those who are well do not need a physician, but the sick do. Go and learn the meaning of the words, 'I desire mercy, not sacrifice.' I did not come to call the righteous but sinners." **Matthew 9:9-13**

Methods of Teaching as Christ Taught in Your Everyday Life

1. Have meals together every day as a family and use the time to talk.
2. Begin your meals with prayer.
3. Write letters and e-mails to children when they are away at camp, college or moving into their own apartments. Apply scripture truths when you have an opportunity to offer advice. Encourage them in their faith walk.
4. Offer a neighbor a ride when her car breaks down.
5. Deliver a meal to a friend when he's sick, pray with him.
6. Offer words of sympathy when someone is grieving a loss.

Applying Biblical Truths Today

Over the years, I have heard a number of people emphatically proclaim that the Bible is an ancient book that's wisdom is no longer applicable today. Time and time again, I hear conversations about how times have changed, the lessons are out-dated and irrelevant. Yet, as I look back over my own life, I can clearly see the frequency in which I could apply valuable lessons from the Bible. In my first book, Refiner's Fire, I provided a number of examples of this.

As in the last book, in this work, I would like to urge daily Bible study to foster spiritual growth in your life. My spiritual journey is not much different from that of other people. After studying the first letter of Paul to the Corinthians, I quickly discovered that my spiritual journey was not much different than that of the Corinthian people two-thousand years ago! After I accepted Jesus as my savior, I continued "in an ordinary human way" (Chapter 3, verse 3) just as they did. But, gradually, the full revelation of the impact of Jesus' crucifixion and resurrection came in a variety of lessons. I learned my lessons the hard way.

As my faith life matured, I began to ask God to show me areas in my life that were not in keeping with His commandments and He did. Failing to follow God's call in my life and failing to forgive were just some of the things that He revealed to me. I resisted God's call to teach in a religious education program when I was in Connecticut and God brought it back to my attention after a series of disasters occurred in connection with the choices that I made to avoid the call to teach. The consequences of my actions were realized almost immediately. I began to read the Bible much more carefully and to seek God's directions more actively. The words of the Bible were not just poetic, idly spoken words; but, rather a revelation of the truth from God. God revealed other areas of my life in which I had failed. Jesus' teaching on prayer in the Gospel of Matthew, Chapter 6 verses 15 and the parable of the lost son in the Gospel of Luke, Chapter 15 verses 11-32 drove home the point of forgiveness as I dealt with the pain of divorce. As I mulled over the fact that I needed to forgive my ex-husband and come to terms with my own role in the demise of our marriage, I realized that in the past I had boldly asked God to forgive me for times that I had sinned yet I refused to forgive someone who hurt me.

It was during this time that I realized that Jesus, innocent of any wrong doing, in fact, free of any sin at all, suffered and died a horrible death thus paying the ultimate price for all of our sins. I remember reading the words of the Gospel of John, Chapter 1, "In the beginning was the Word, and the Word was with God, and the Word was God. He was in the beginning with God. All things came to be through him, and without him nothing came to be." All of a sudden, the meaning of the cross in my life became clear. Jesus loved us so much that He sacrificed Himself. Jesus was God incarnate! How then could I hold on to past hurts and remain unforgiving? How could I continue to make unloving choices? How could I continue to ignore God's call in my life? It was not that I had never heard this word of truth before. I had, many times. But, it did not resonate within my soul until I recognized my own failings and made the connection that Jesus was, indeed, God. I also had to come to the conclusion that nothing I could do or say could produce salvation. Only Jesus can save me. Alleluia!

After that, the words of John 3:16-17 made more sense, "For God so loved the world that he gave his only Son, so that everyone who believes in him might not perish but might have eternal life. For God did not send his son into the world to condemn the world, but that that the world might be saved through him."

Jesus' Resurrection opens the door for eternal life—something that is impossible for us to accomplish without Him for we all are stained from sin; yet, He forgives us. He died for us and rose from the dead. Thanks to Jesus, we, too, will have life after death.

As I continued my study, I began to examine the things that Paul brought to the Corinthian people's attention. Some of the areas that Paul spoke of, I felt that I had already experienced tremendous growth. For example, Paul dealt heavily with the topic of love in Chapter 13. At one time in my life, my perception of love was distorted by worldly ideas and my relationships suffered because of it. But, as I began to test my idea of love against the holy word of God, I realized that most of the time I was experiencing something else. The words lust and jealousy seemed more appropriate. I knew I had to work on this area in my life. I have worked on this and my relationships have improved.

Yet, when I read the words in Chapter 10, verse 10, "Do not grumble as some of them did and suffered death by the destroyer," I felt the prick of recognition in myself and I realized that I still needed to work on this area in my life. How many times have I grumbled about various trials in my life and failed to trust in the Lord? I realized that this was an important lesson that I needed to face. I found comfort in the words just a few lines later, "God is faithful and will not let you be tried beyond your strength; but, with the trial he will also provide a way out so that you may be able to bear it." I believe the Lord has been challenging me to be more attentive to this lesson.

Recently, as I took a class on the book of Exodus, I saw how the Israelites grumbled and complained as God led them out of Egypt to the Promised Land. They complained about the lack of food, the lack of water and the miserable conditions in the desert; yet, they failed to see that God was leading them out of the bondage of slavery. The same prick of recognition came and I knew once again that God was still teaching and working on me in this area. While I have improved, it is still a tough lesson to learn. We need to train ourselves to rely on God's love.

Death in Me, for Life in You

Our study at church on the Second Letter of Paul to the Corinthian people produced a number of opportunities for me to dig deeper, to really look for opportunities for growth. Wes Clemmer was our instructor for one of those classes. His assignment for us after studying Paul's words was to pray for an opportunity for "death in me for life in you". This is a hard concept because no one *wants* to die. Jesus sacrificed himself for us. It was a painful, physical sacrifice. The sacrifice that we were talking about in class was not necessarily a physical sacrifice; but, rather, a letting go of the need to take care of oneself first. It was putting our needs, wants and desires on hold or letting go of them to reach out and to take care of the needs of someone else.

I immediately began to pray for this opportunity. I wondered aloud to my sister Bobby on Sunday morning if the opportunity would come in a couple of weeks instead of by Wednesday night when the assignment was due. I had not seen any results to my prayer, as yet. But, later that same day, I was reminded that God's timing is perfect.

The pastors of Grace Covenant Church encourage their members to become part of a life-group so that you can enjoy fellowship with other Christians as well as have an opportunity to share spiritual gifts with one another for the edification of the people and to provide love, support and companionship to one another. Our life group generally meets on Sunday afternoon. On this particular Sunday, we were scheduled to meet at 3:00 p.m. Generally, our life-group meetings are 2 to 2 ½ hours in length. The meeting was at my house as Barbara Mannino, our life group leader, had asked me to lead the group discussion. I had an out-line prepared so that we would have plenty of conversation starters as well as scripture readings to apply and to discuss. Figuring that we would be finished by 5:00 or 5:30 p.m., after the meeting, I planned to go to the pharmacy to pick up a prescription, visit my mother, do laundry, do some on-line research—well, you get the idea. I had an agenda, a list of things to accomplish. It was a schedule that I intended to adhere to. My plans were changed, however, when one of the women clearly needed to talk. She asked for prayer. Barbara counseled the woman at length and we all prayed for her. The afternoon evaporated quickly and soon much of the evening dried up right along with it. The meeting did not end until nearly 9:00 p.m. Not one item on my list of things to do could be crossed off.

I realized immediately that this was an example of dying to self for life in others. My rigid agenda had to bend, had to actually give way, to help this woman. The spirit moves at the proper time whether it fit my schedule or not. The needs of this woman were more important than any schedule. It was important for me to see this principle in action. I wondered how many times I have missed opportunities to reach out to others because my eyes were fixed on what was next on my list of things to accomplish. While it is good to be organized and have a plan, one must also be flexible enough to reach out to those around us even when it is not on the list. Had I been missing opportunities to reach out to others and to share the love of God with others? Most likely, yes!

Realizing what Jesus sacrificed for us, relinquishing plans is really a small sacrifice. But, how often do we cling to things that we think are important? It was a good lesson for me.

Being open to the move of the Holy Spirit is a key component to Christian life. I praise and thank God for helping me to let go of my need to stay on schedule all the time.

As I look back on other instances in my life where I was running from appointment to appointment, one errand to another, I can clearly see that I was not taking the time to open my eyes to the people around me. When I was delayed in line at the grocery store, did I miss an opportunity to speak to someone about the love of Christ because I was too absorbed in looking at my list of things to do or checking my cell phone for the time? When I took Pepper for her walk when I got home did I miss an opportunity to minister to my elderly neighbor by just waving at him and marching the dog up and down the sidewalk out of routine?

He indeed died for all, so that those who live might no longer live for themselves but for him who for their sake died and was raised. **2 Corinthians 5:15**

Integrity

In reflecting on the value of integrity, I recall an incident that occurred while I was the director of Confirmation. I was not only the director of the program but a teacher as well. Also teaching in my program was a nun. Two boys in her class were joking around and not paying much attention to her; so, she threw them out of the class. The boys came to me shaken and apologetic. They readily admitted that they had not behaved properly and asked for forgiveness. Sister stopped by my office later and told me that she did not think that they deserved a second chance.

My heart broke for these boys because I sensed sincerity in their voices. Yet, I did not want to undermine Sister's authority over her classroom by reversing a call that she had made. But, when I looked in their eyes, I saw defeat. They really were sorry. I am sure they were thinking that because Sister was a religious nun her words would have a lot of impact on my decision about their fate in attending Confirmation classes. The truth was that I valued her opinion very much and respected her authority. I mulled the situation over carefully. I read to them the Parable of the Unforgiving Servants in Matthew 18:21-35. I realized that my response to their behavior had to line up with the teachings of Christ, otherwise the integrity of the entire program would be called into question. If our words and actions do not match what we teach, then how could we expect these young people to grow in their faith and learn about the love of Jesus. I explained to the boys that their behavior in class was wrong; but, I forgave them and told them they could attend classes with the understanding that they were in class to learn and not to be disruptive. I ended up talking with both of the boy's mothers as well.

Sister was stunned when I told her that the boys would be allowed to continue to attend class, only they would be in my class. Initially, she was not very happy about my decision. I am not sure if she felt that my solution somehow diminished her authority or excused poor behavior; but, I explained my reason and how I had discussed their behavior, clearly pointing out that it had been unacceptable.

The boys flourished in class and we watched them transform from cantankerous teenagers to mature young men. I shudder to think what message they would have gotten had I refused to accept their apologies.

A year later, I was pleased when the boys received the Sacrament of Confirmation. They were really ready to accept the Baptism of the Holy Spirit. That night, they both thanked me for accepting their apology and letting them continue with their spiritual studies. Just a few months later, one of the young men suffered a tremendous loss. His older brother was killed in a car crash. I had taught his brother in Confirmation class, too. It was a heart-wrenching experience. After I spent a few minutes with the young man at the wake, I remember watching him comforting some of his brother's friends as they grieved. He put aside his own grief to be a comfort to them. He was truly walking in faith. I knew the Lord's hand was upon him. Oh, how he had grown, praise the Lord!

*Then Peter approaching asked him, "Lord, if my brother sins against me, how often must I forgive him? As man as seven times?" Jesus answered, "I say to you, not seven times but seventy-seven times." **Matthew 18:21-22***

Building Blocks

Have you ever played the game Jenga? If you have, you know that it is a game in which the players build a tower of red, blue and yellow blocks. Play begins with the youngest player rolling a color cube. The player must then find a block of the same color that he rolled and pull it out of the tower. As you can imagine, as play goes on, the game becomes more and more difficult. The game ends when someone pulls a block from the tower and the tower comes tumbling down. The player who was the last one to successfully pull a block from the tower without toppling it wins. One can easily see how important a firm foundation is when blocks are being pulled from various parts of the building.

Alas, our life is much the same. When various trials and troubles come into our lives, if we have a firm foundation built with Jesus as the cornerstone, we can withstand the difficulties that come our way. Building our life on biblical truths and principles will gives us that solid base that we all need. Some of our building blocks, to name a few, are faith, love, prayer, scripture study, God's commandments, and tithing. Naturally, none of us would purposefully pull out a building block and cause the tower (our life) to come crashing down. But, some of us do just that. We pick and choose the principles that are taught in the Bible, utilizing the ones we are comfortable with and skipping the ones that make us a little uneasy. Take some time to reflect on what building blocks you are using in your life. Are you pulling out important building blocks in your life?

The comparisons to the game go much deeper. If you think about the strategy in the game, a wise player will pick blocks to pull out that will destabilize the building for the next player. Quite often, this is exactly what happens in our daily lives either wittingly or unwittingly. How many times have the actions of others compromised your own situation? You can be enjoying stability (happiness) one day, and the next day, find yourself, living precariously (fearful, angry).

In reality, the winner in life is not the one who pulls out building blocks of life. The truth is that the winner in life is the one who realizes that Jesus is the cornerstone, the very foundation of our lives. It is He who preserves life.

Think of situations in your life where you may be destabilizing your foundation. Do you allow unforgiveness to reign in your heart? Do you tend to broil with anger when disagreements arise or when you are wronged? Do you try to find ways to justify telling a lie? Do you think its o.k. to take office supplies from your employer? Do you use profanity? Have you ever put down or hurt someone else in the workplace to get ahead or make yourself look better? Do you frequently find yourself holding back on contributions at church or to charitable causes? Do you avoid spending time with Christian friends to avoid spiritual conversations that may cause you to confront a belief that is not in-line with the teachings of Christ (i.e. abortion, homosexuality).

"Build up, build up, prepare the way, remove the stumbling blocks from my people's path." **Isaiah 57:14**

That's Life

Many of you are familiar with the Frank Sinatra song, *That's Life*. Sinatra croons the lyrics, "I've been up and down and over and out, and I know one thing, each time I find myself layin' flat on my face, I just pick myself up and get back in the race." I have a fondness for this song that I never had before because I have heard my friend, Matt Bernardi, sing this song at karaoke. He really has a great singing voice; so, it is always enjoyable to hear him sing. "That's Life" is one of his best numbers.

When I hear this song, I am also aware of a stark reality in life and that is that we all know that sometimes it just isn't that easy to pick ourselves up after a painful experience and get on with our lives. We also know that we cannot do it ourselves. As followers of Jesus, we know we have a Source of Comfort and a Healer. We have found out that, as the song says, "Some people get their kicks stompin' on our dreams". But, when we are a part of a community of believers who love Jesus, we find encouragement and support for our dreams.

One of the special features of being a part of Grace Covenant Church in Lewistown, Pennsylvania, is getting connected with a Life Group. As I said earlier, Life Groups meet regularly to provide fellowship for believers and allow opportunities to encourage one another, support each other and love each other as we encounter the joys and trials of life. So, as Sinatra sings, "don't let it, let it get down you down", one can find solace in connecting with a life group and enjoying life to the fullest. Even if your church does not offer life groups, make it a point to spend time with like-minded Christians who can listen with a compassionate heart and can help you apply the truths of the Bible to everyday life. Spend time with people who know and understand spiritual gifts and use them.

We are bombarded by secular thinking every single day. Television programs and advertisements promote all kinds of products, theories, advice and so forth that can lead us away from turning to Our Creator for the answers to life's most difficult questions and circumstances. When we align ourselves with a strong, Bible based church, we can find ourselves on the way to joyful, peaceful living. Does that mean we will never face troubles again? No, but, it does mean when trials and difficulties arise, we will have the love and support of our Loving Father and a group of people who will guide, comfort and assist us.

So, the next time you hear someone sing or say, "That's Life!", you can say, "Yes, and it's a good life through Jesus Christ!"

He said to [his] disciples, "Therefore I tell you, do not worry about your life and what you will eat, or about your body and what you will wear."
Luke 12:22-23

Spirituality at the Racetrack

For many years, I have been a great fan of car racing, especially NASCAR. From the beginning of his career, I rooted for Rusty Wallace. I tuned in to the Sunday race, previously known as the Winston Cup race, now known as the Nextel Cup, to follow the race from start to finish. It was my way of relaxing. Everyone who knew me came to know how much of a fan I was. In fact, most people knew not to call me during a race. Occasionally, I would get a call from my sister or a friend during a commercial to comment on something that took place on the track. But, lengthy conversations, no way! When I could get away, I would go to races with my sister, Bobby, and/or other friends who loved car racing. We would have a grand time standing on pit road during qualifying, visiting the souvenir trailers, watching practice sessions, and then enjoying the main event on Sunday. The drivers and their crews became a sort of extended family to me. While I had my favorites, there were very few that I didn't like.

One thing I enjoyed about going to the track was getting to the track early, getting myself a hot cup of coffee at one of the food stands, and sitting on the grandstand to await the first rumble of an engine being fired up. During that quiet time, I could spend time in prayer. My sister and I both took our Bibles to the track and could even work in some Bible study when there weren't cars on the track. I remember one time when my sister was doing her daily devotional one morning at the Pocono Speedway at Long Pond, Pennsylvania, a race fan stopped to remark about her taking the time to do her devotions. They had a pleasant exchange about it. It was an excellent opportunity to set an example for others, too.

My friend Cathy and I attended a NASCAR event at the Bristol Motor Speedway in Bristol, Tennessee. I have a great fondness for this track as I once lived in Bristol. So, attending the race there many years later turned out to be a great treat for me. But, one of my fondest memories from there did not happen on the ½ mile high banked oval. It happened instead on the drag strip where the Sunday morning Christian church service was celebrated. Cathy and I sat on the bleachers and listened to an awesome group singing Christian music. We, then, got to hear a phenomenal Baptist preacher deliver one of the best sermons I've ever heard.

The other thing I love about NASCAR races is that before each event there is time allowed before the National Anthem for prayer. It's awesome to see thousands of heads bowed to take time to speak to the Lord our God before enjoying a sporting event. With thanks and praise offered, petitions made for the protection of the drivers, crews and fans assembled, it is beautiful testimony for those in the crowd or someone watching on television who may not be a believer to see and to hear.

So, from the dynamic preaching of a Southern Baptist at Bristol Motor Speedway to a Catholic Mass celebrated at victory circle at the Pocono International Speedway, I've had an opportunity to praise and worship God while enjoying my favorite sport. Whether at Richmond, Bristol, Pocono, or Nazareth, I've spent time in prayer and in the Word of God while enjoying a race. I've watched drivers jump out of their cars in victory circle and remember to thank God first. I've seen drivers who taped scripture passages to their dashboards, too. These are role models that I would be happy for my children to look up to.

Race fans also know that there is more to racing than cars rocketing around an oval at 180 mph. Even people tuning into a televised race for the first time soon realize that the crews have done a great deal of work back at the shop to get the car ready, pit crews need to perform their work quickly and efficiently at every pit stop and crew chiefs and drivers must make split second decisions to adapt to rapidly changing conditions. The drivers need to have a great deal of faith in their crew chiefs to get behind the wheel and have the confidence to race at such a high rate of speed. They also have to have great communication between them at all times so that they can constantly work toward making their performance better.

In daily living, we need to rely on our Creator, God the Father, for provision, guidance and care. Trusting Him, as we take each day, sometimes having to make hard decisions, sometimes facing distractions and disasters, we can be assured that we move forward. Knowing that God is the Master Mechanic in our life, the One who has the best plan for us, we are well equipped for each day. When we relax and let God be our crew chief and take charge of our lives, we can face the "race" ahead of us. In Paul's first letter to the Corinthians in chapter 9, he uses a different kind of racing analogy to make his point. We can take his advice today. "Run so as to win". Race car drivers enter every race with the intention of winning. We should do the same with our lives with God as our crew chief, running the race by His (God's rules) and with His guidance. If we don't live our lives well, we'll get black flagged. (That means there will be penalties.) If we've done well, we'll see God waving a checkered flag for us. (Hey, that means, we won!)

*"Therefore, since we are surrounded by so great a cloud of witnesses, let us rid ourselves of every burden and sin that clings to us and persevere in running the race that lies before us while keeping our eyes fixed on Jesus, the leader and perfecter of faith." **Hebrews 12:1-2***

The Hand of God upon Me

As I have become more familiar with how God speaks to His people by reading the Bible, I can look back on my own life and clearly see God's hand upon me, guiding me and directing me. It is easy to look at the lives of other believers and see how God has worked in their lives, as well.

On four occasions, I have seen God's hand in placing me in specific jobs for a specific purpose. I would like to share these circumstances with you in this chapter. Even now after living through the experiences myself, I am still awed at how God managed to work out every detail and corrected me on one occasion when I foolishly tried to avoid His call on my life.

The first occasion was when I became the parish secretary at Saint Louis Church in West Haven, Connecticut. It was an ordinary Sunday. I went to Mass, as usual, and sat near the front. But, something happened that day that would change my life. I went forward to receive Holy Communion. As Father Peter offered me the Eucharist, I saw a twinkle in his eye. At that instant, I knew that something was up. So, after Mass, as I shook Father Peter's hand, I was not at all surprised when he asked me to call him Monday morning. On the way home, I wondered if there was a project he wanted me to work on for the church or a committee he wanted me to organize. When I called on Monday morning, Father Peter asked me if I knew anything about computers. Since I had done data entry and word processing in previous jobs, I told him that I was fairly well versed in computer work. He asked me to come work for him. He was interested in getting the parish files into a computer data base to streamline the office work. I told him that I could do it. The assistant pastor at that time was Father Eugene Charman. He was the computer whiz for the Archdiocese of Hartford and was helping a lot of parishes to modernize their offices. So, with his help in finding the right program, we began the task of getting the parish data into the computer. It took a few months; but, we did it. Before long, my part-time job turned into a full-time job when the parish secretary wanted to cut down her hours to part-time. Father Peter asked me to take on that responsibility and I did.

Several times, I heard Father Peter tell people how he felt that the Holy Spirit had directed him to ask me to come to work at the rectory. He did not know my background at all. All he knew about me was that I attended Mass regularly and had young children at home. He delighted in telling people that when I came up for Communion that day in church, he felt a prompting from the Holy Spirit, a knowing from within, that I was the person that he should ask to fulfill the role. I had recognized the moment as well even though I didn't really know what it was about. That moment launched eighteen years of service for one of the most challenging yet fulfilling jobs I've ever held.

The second occasion was when our Director of Religious Education stepped down. Father Peter interviewed a couple of people for the job; yet, neither person seemed quite right. At the time, my divorce had become final and it was abundantly clear that I was not going to be able to make ends meet on my salary. I would need a second job. Father Peter and I talked at length about the attributes the person in charge of instructing the children of the parish in the faith should have. After a pause, Father Peter asked me if I would be willing to take the job. I agreed. I loved working with the children and the teachers in our program. It turned out to be a rewarding, rich experience. Not only did the children grow in their faith; but, I grew as well. I could not help but to think about the time that I had taught Sunday School in the Lutheran Church. I was returning to the kind of work that I had done during and immediately after high school. I also recalled the conversation I had with Monsignor Pitoniak when my daughter Carissa was just a baby. He had encouraged me, then, to think about teaching.

I nearly blew it with the third opportunity that the Lord arranged for me. Three of the five Catholic churches in West Haven were looking for a Confirmation director. I was already running the Confirmation program at Saint Louis Church; so, Father Peter didn't really feel compelled to join forces with the other churches. He felt we had a solid program that did not need adjustment. One of the pastors in town asked if I would be interested in the Confirmation job. A part of me was interested. In fact, a desire to do the job flared up inside me; but, I declined because I was contemplating moving to North Carolina. It didn't really fit in my plans for the future; so, I backed away from it. Well, truthfully, it was a moment of disobedience for which I am not proud. My plans to move to North Carolina rapidly unraveled. I shared this story at length in my first book, *Refiner's Fire.* I was a modern day Jonah, stubbornly refusing to do what God had called me to do. So, when the opportunity resurfaced after the man that was hired didn't stay on, I knew that God had brought the opportunity back in front of me. I called the priests involved to tell them that I was interested and was hired. The job required a lot of work and could be frustrating at times. Yet, it was so rewarding. Seeing the teens grow in their love for the Lord was awesome and to be able to play a role in their development was a fantastic opportunity to fulfill God's call.

The fourth opportunity that God arranged for me was my job at CVS. While I had never worked in retail, I know that the Lord planted me there for a reason. After I moved from Connecticut to Pennsylvania, the Lord provided a sufficient delay in finding a job for me so that I could accomplish the writing I was called to do. Upon completion of the spiritual book, I landed the job at CVS. Imagine my delight when I realized that God had put me in a position to learn about a publisher and then have the publisher accept my work! God is an awesome God, isn't He? In addition, he put me in a position where I got to meet a lot of people. I made new friends and learned new skills.

I also saw something that, perhaps at first, I didn't want to see. For quite awhile I could not see why I could not seem to be finding an office job. After all, for years, I had performed secretarial work. Not only did I enjoy it and feel comfortable doing the job, I also received many compliments on my performance. I began to question why I needed to be on my feet all day in a retail position. I even contemplated changing jobs and actively looked for office work. But, I suddenly realized that I was in the public eye among many people from all walks of life. I had an endless stream of people in front of me every day. I realized that my training had not been limited to office work but included teaching as well. The Lord began to impress upon me the importance of being seen in the workplace, walking and talking as a Christian. It was quite clear to me that the Lord did not want me hidden behind a desk any longer with limited contact with people. My call included mixing with people and not just people who already had a relationship with God.

The periods of preparation in my life have brought me to this moment. The experiences that I have had have put me in a unique position to be able to impart wisdom to others, to share the gifts and talents that God has given to me and to be able to deepen my own relationship with God all at the same time. Without a doubt, I know that God has more in store for me. I can see that God has surrounded me with a number of wonderful friends, each one with a gifting that will be interlocked with my gifts to fulfill God's purpose. There are times when I don't feel worthy of this call; yet, I know that if God has called me, He thinks I'm worthy and that's all that matters. There are times when I think that I don't have the necessary credentials; yet, if God has called me, he has equipped me with the Holy Spirit, the only credential necessary to complete the task.

With my own desire to follow the will of God, I have begun to see how important it is to help others with their quest to follow God's call. This is why opportunities for fellowship with other Christians is vital to our spiritual growth.

Think of it this way. For most of us, when we hear the telephone ring, we feel compelled to answer it. There is no doubt that the majority of people find it nearly impossible to ignore a ringing telephone. Even people who have gotten caller id service in their homes, out of frustration from relentless calls from telemarketers, will get up to check to see who is calling. When we miss a call, we often find ourselves wondering who it was or if it was regarding something important.

Other people don't seem to find it all that necessary to rush to the phone to see who it is. These folks are content to sit back and let the phone ring. They are satisfied to let others find out who is calling and what the call is about. Still others take it even farther; they will avoid getting on the phone at all costs. Even if the call is for them, they don't want to take the call. They don't want to get involved or interact with anyone.

When God calls, how do you respond? We are all called to do the work of the Lord in some capacity. Whether it is reaching out in love to our brothers and sisters in day to day activities or if it is stepping into a specific ministry, we all have a purpose and a plan, a call, for our lives. Are you ready to answer the call or are you waiting for someone else to answer. Let's be like young Samuel in 1 Samuel 1:10 after he was instructed that God was calling him and let our response be, "Speak, Lord, your servant is listening."

God has created each of us to be a unique individual. We each have a plan and a purpose according to God's perfect will for our lives. We often hear people proclaiming our freedom to choose and that we are in charge of our own destinies. This declaration is especially prominent in the United States where we have become accustomed to a number of rights and freedoms that people in other countries do not have. While it is true that we do have a choice, we must remind ourselves that there are right and wrong choices. If you make a wrong choice, there are consequences. Many people can make this connection with regard to sinful choices, right and wrong, in terms of murder, stealing and acts that are clearly harmful to self and to others. Yet, quite often, we don't want to think about this in terms of our choice to follow God's call and to follow the promptings of the Holy Spirit.

We can choose to follow or not. This is true. For example, someone called to teach may choose instead to sit behind the scenes. When we make choices like this, it's just like wearing someone else's shoes. They just don't seem to fit quite right. If the shoes are too big, they fall off your feet causing your steps to be awkward. If the shoes are too small, you might not even be able to get them on or, if you do get them on, they cause you great pain. Even if you borrow someone else's shoes and they do fit, eventually, you have to give them back.

God chose you for a purpose before the world ever began. It's easier and more enjoyable to follow the path that He has set for you. It is only when you are being You that you can release your full potential and enjoy the true prosperity in every area of your life that God has prepared for you to enjoy.

Romans 8:28 (NIV) says this: "And we know that in all things God works for the good of those who love him, who have been called according to His purpose."

If you feel like your shoes don't fit today, ask God for direction. When you've reached the place when you're doing what you are called to do, you will feel a sense of joy, peace and comfort. While you still may find yourself tired (and yes, even a good pair of shoes can pinch your toes by the end of the day), you will know in your heart that you are fulfilling your purpose, the purpose for which God made and prepared you.

As always, our hindsight is 20/20. But, we must train ourselves to have 20/20 vision in the present when it comes to God's direction and provision in our lives. When I look back over my life, I can clearly see God's hand upon me.

Ten years before the life-altering fire in my home, I had a dream that the house burned. The dream had left such a profound impression upon me that I suffered from paranoia for a long time. I became obsessive about making sure the coffee pot was not only turned off but unplugged when I left the house. I was extraordinarily careful about candles and frequently checked power cords for splits and frays. But, as time wore on, the impact of the dream began to fade. That is, until the night of the fire. When I stood with the fire fighters inside the blackened, burned out shell that was once the upstairs of my home, the memory of the dream came back in a flash. What I was seeing was exactly how it was in my dream, ten years earlier. I realized in an instant that God had shown me a window into the future. As I experienced the revelation of the spiritual significance of this life changing event in my life and the life of my son, I learned and grew. I came to know a number of truths about God.

God's hand was upon me and my son all the time. It was His way of telling me I know what's going on and I know how it will be resolved. At the time of the dream, I had no inkling of the trouble that my son would encounter. It was unknown to me; but, known by God, that Tim had already come under the influence of the crowd that he was hanging out with at the time. The ball was already in motion. Things were already beginning to go awry.

God speaks to us through a variety of methods. Dreams are just one. In my first book, Refiner's Fire, I share a story about my efforts to make a move to North Carolina. As I backed out of my driveway, I heard a voice sound in my ear that told me that this was not a good time to go to North Carolina. It was as clear as though there were a passenger in my car speaking to me. Yet, I was alone. I ignored that voice and three hours later my car had a blown engine leaving me stranded in Pennsylvania late at night.

It is imperative that we train ourselves and our children to learn to recognize the hand of God in our lives and listen to the instruction that is provided. The dream of the fire was not intended to show me how to avoid it; but, rather to show me that it had a purpose.

The audible voice in the car was indeed a warning. For some time, I was haunted by this. I knew it was important yet, when I had the chance to talk about what happened, I discovered that I was not expressing the reality of what happened I would say, "I heard a voice sound in my ears that told me that this was not a good time to go to North Carolina. I chose to ignore it." Now, I say, "I chose to ignore Him." This is the truth. I stubbornly and disobediently chose to ignore a direct instruction from God. It was truly a humbling experience for me. We all have done this at some point. We make our disobedience sound like it was a misstep or a poor choice.

Pepper

God has allowed me to be the care taker of a beautiful black and white cocker spaniel. I call her Pepper because her predominant color is black. Her official AKC papers states her name as "Salt and Pepper"; but, I call her Pepper for short. We have been through thick and thin together. When I think back at some of the things that we have gone through together, I laugh because she has the ability to bring a smile to my face with her playful, good natured romping. Other times, she can bring a tear to my eye when she shows her soft, compassionate side, cuddling in for some loving when I haven't had such a great day. She just seems to know when it's appropriate to lick my face or just crawl into my lap. There have been times, too, when I've beamed with pride when she fearlessly faced a situation when she knew I, or someone else, was afraid. Those of you that read my first book will recall that she was my hero when she caught the horrible rat that had gotten into my home and had wrecked havoc on my peace when I was living in Connecticut. She also saved the day for my sister when she was spending some time with her. She caught a bat that had gotten into her house. How amazing and awesome it is that a twenty pound dog could fearlessly take care of these problems. She is now twelve years old. I have to say that she has been the finest companion dog I have ever had.

I have learned a lot from my relationship with my sweet little friend. She has been a remarkable example of how important it is to rely on our God, our Master.

As Pepper's master, I am in charge. She is obedient to my command. If she did not listen to my commands to stay, she could find herself wandering into trouble (a busy street, the neighbor's yard where a pit bull is housed). Pepper has demonstrated her obedience skills time and time again.

One day I observed her do something that struck me as incredibly interesting. I had gone up the stairs to retrieve something from my bedroom. It only took me a couple of moments to find what I needed and I returned to the staircase. Pepper was waiting patiently at the bottom of the stairs. That seemed very interesting to me because usually she follows me wherever I go. Then, I realized that she had waited to see if I was coming back down right away or if I was going to say on the second floor for awhile. The next time I went up the staircase I realized that she consistently watched my movements to determine whether or not she should follow. Apparently, turning off lights on the first floor was a pretty good indicator to her that we were going upstairs for the night and she would happily march up the stairs next to me. She also seems to know that if I take certain things like my Bible or my purse that these are good indicators that it won't be a short stay on the second floor. It is truly remarkable to me that she has become so very observant of my every move and even waits patiently to see what my next move will be.

After making this observation, I realized that our relationship with God needs to work the same way. We need to patiently watch for God's move in our lives and take our steps according to His movements. I thought of it this way. Had Pepper darted up the stairs with me only to discover that I was going to return to the first floor moments later, she would have expended a lot of energy unnecessarily. Her steps would have been wasted. Sometimes we do the very same thing. We try to rush into situations without allowing God to do His work ahead of us. How many times do we rush after things without waiting to see God's move in our lives? There are times that we actually interfere with the work that God must do to prepare a situation before we get involved in it.

Flip Flops

Sometimes when God speaks to His people, He uses pictures instead of words to illustrate His point. Quite often, it is something that stands out vividly in order to get our attention. I have had this happen many times. Sometimes, I don't immediately understand the meaning of the picture. Our human mind wants to analyze things. In this case, the temptation is to try to decipher the meaning using logic and reason. But, all we really need to do is ask the Lord to tell us what it means. The Lord our God will give us the answer directly.

There are times when the word is intended just for me and other times it is meant to be shared with a specific person or sometimes many people in a group setting. It took me some time to let go of my humanity enough to know the difference. My tendency, at first, was to hold back and keep the information to myself. A part of me figured that if God was speaking to me it had to do with me. But, then, as I matured as a Christian, I began to think less of myself and more in terms of how I could help others grow in their love for the Lord. Initially, I held back for fear that someone would think that my message or interpretation didn't make any sense. Once again, I was looking at it from a purely human perspective. Then, with encouragement from mature Christians, I came to realize that I needed to get out of the way and allow the Spirit to work. I was just to be a vessel, an instrument. All I needed to do was just follow the prompting of the Spirit. There was no need to worry about anything. Subsequently, I realized that when I remained in a prayerful state, it was very clear when the message was to be shared and when it was not intended for a larger audience. Throughout the Bible, in the Old Testament and New Testament, God gave those that he called the necessary words and provisions to accomplish the mission they were given. There is no reason for us to think that God would not do the same for us.

I would like to share an example of a word that God gave me that I believe was intended for more people than just myself. I have shared this with a number of people and have been amazed at how often people will remark that it struck a chord deep within their souls as though the message was intended specifically for them.

In the morning and again in the late evening, I try to spend time reading and reflecting on scripture passages and then sitting in a quiet place to talk to God. As I mentioned earlier, I love to sit on the front porch of my home with a hot cup of coffee in the morning. The morning sun feels good and puts me in a peaceful, comfortable state. The quietness of an early morning hour also provides fewer distractions so that I can listen for and clearly hear God speak to me. Enjoying the beauty of creation and reading the Holy Bible is a great way to start any day. I also enjoy curling up in a comfortable chair in the evening for more study and prayer. With my dog at my side and my Bible in hand, I find it is the loveliest way to conclude the day.

One particular morning, after a time of prayer, an image of a pair of flip-flops kept coming to mind. Yes, you read that correctly, a pair of flip flops. I wondered about this as I gazed down at my feet clad in, you guessed it, a pair of flip flops. I was sure that I had allowed my mind to wander. I tried to re-focus my thoughts to God and there they were again. Flip flops. So, I said out loud, "Lord, what do these flip flops mean?"

I found myself thinking about the 2004 Republican Convention when Vice President Dick Cheney made his memorable speech in which he referred to Presidential candidate Senator John Kerry as a flip-flopper, someone who changed his stance on issues numerous times. I found myself laughing out loud as I recalled the crowd of conventioneers waving their flip flops and chanting "Flip-Flop" "Flip Flop". Whether you agreed with Dick Cheney's speech or not, you would have to agree that it was an excellent speech. He not only made his point; but, he crafted it in such a way that his speech would be remembered.

Well, the meaning of the Lord's message just about hit me over the head. It was so clear.

I felt the Lord speak into my heart that day. He told me that people often change their stance on Christian principles, moral issues and beliefs according to their own situation. I began to think back to times in my own life when I may have become a cafeteria Christian, picking and choosing principles that worked for me and ignoring the ones that I found hard to accept. I still shudder at some of the choices I made as a young woman. Despite the fact that I was brought up in a Christian home, I still chose to say and do things that did not line up with Christian teachings. As I matured as a Christian, I began to realize that I had to abide by all God's commandments, not just part of it. I often ask God to show me areas in my life that I need to work on. He does.

There was a time in my life when I struggled with the principle of tithing. I would look at the bills and then look at my income. Human logic and reason would whisper to me that if I didn't put so much in my church envelope this week I could pay another bill. I've had to learn how to let go of my finances and let God take over. The more I thought about it, the more I realized that the Flip-flop message was intended for all of us. We've all done it and will be tempted to do it in the future. We must remain anchored to God to stabilize our footing lest we fall into the trap of deception the enemy has in store for us.

What other ways do we "Flip-Flop"? Sometimes, we flip-flop in our prayer life. We talk to God about a situation and ask for favor in it. Then, the very next day, we change our minds and move on to another situation in which to ask for favor. We are constantly shifting our thoughts from one project to another, abandoning goals and setting new ones, only to change again and again. Again, flip-flop, flip-flop. Take some time to think about this and you will be amazed when the Lord brings to your attention times that you were a flip-flopper.

Personal Revival

For many of us, when we return home after a long, hard day at work or even after an exhausting journey, we need time to recover before we can actually relax for the evening.

Whether it is sitting on the front porch with a glass of ice tea or easing into an overstuffed chair in the living room, our minds and bodies need an opportunity to disconnect from the days events. When we don't take time to recuperate, our minds continue to try to solve work day problems and our bodies refuse to relax. I can think of a number of times when I came home from work and jumped right into cleaning and cooking without taking a few minutes to decompress. My mind replayed the upsetting telephone call I had taken at the beginning of the day. A review of the day's ups and downs played like a movie in the back of my mind. Before I knew it, I was already thinking ahead to tomorrow's agenda while cutting the vegetables for the evening meal. Ordinarily, I enjoyed cooking; but, now the preparation seemed to be taking more energy than I could muster. What was usually a joy was looking more like drudgery.

When we do take the time to revive ourselves, we feel refreshed and reenergized and can enjoy our evening meal, time with our family or even a hobby. I've trained myself to allow myself some time to let go of the day and embrace the evening. I change my clothes, wash my face, and get myself a nice cup of tea or a cool drink. I take a little walk with the dog—sit with my feet up and listen to some music or read a couple chapters in a good book. Once my mind has made the transition from work time to play time, then I turn my attention to preparing dinner. Now, the "joy of cooking" can be appreciated. Meals taste better, family conversation is more relaxed, and my time at home is truly something to look forward to.

Our spiritual lives often need to experience revival, too. When we don't take time for prayer, Bible study and fellowship with other

Christians, we become weary and cannot experience the peace God wants us all to enjoy. When we do take the time to revive ourselves spiritually, the joy and peace of God refreshes us to the very core of our being.

How do we experience personal revival? Taking the time to examine our consciences, confessing our sins, carefully studying the bible and applying biblical principles to daily life, and sharing fellowship with other Christians for friendship and accountability are just a few. But, for the times that we find ourselves going through the motions of being a Christian, we may have to do more. If you find yourself going to church every Sunday and volunteering at the soup kitchen every Saturday; but, don't feel joy in your life, you need personal revival.

Then the peace of God which surpasses all understanding
will guard your hearts and minds in Christ Jesus.
Phillipians 4:7

Opening the Doors and Windows During Life's Storms

Many of my friends have told me that they are amazed that I have maintained a highly optimistic attitude and have a happy disposition despite some of the difficult situations that I have been through. Countless people have said to me, "you always seem so happy". I attribute the ability to stay positive and to be happy despite it all to my relationship with the Lord. I can move through life with peace and strength and courage through the power of the Holy Spirit. By allowing the Holy Spirit to work in me and through me, past hurts are healed and opportunities for the future appear.

Recently, I was on my way to my former father-in-law's funeral in Connecticut when I had a revelation from the Holy Spirit, offering an analogy on how healing of past hurts occurs. My daughter had called to tell me that her grandfather had died. It did not take me very long to decide that I wanted to attend the wake and the funeral. After all, this man had been an important part of my life for a long time and was the grandfather of my children. In addition, I wanted to express my sympathy to my former in-laws, all of them. But, it was also important to me to express my sympathy to my former husband, a man I love with all my heart. He would be hurting and mourning a major loss. I had to be there for our children *and* for him.

So, while I was driving, I prayed for peace and comfort for the family. I'm sure the enemy wanted me to dwell on how uncomfortable it would be for me to be there alone at the wake while my former husband stood with his pregnant wife at his side. But, instead, I chose to send thoughts of love. I was feeling rather emotional on my drive. The death of a loved one is hard. When I had spoken to my daughter and my son on the telephone, I could hear the emotion in their voices. Donald Hussey was a big man with a big heart. When I first met him, I admit I was somewhat intimidated. He was a formidable man. But, as I got to know him, I saw a softer side and I realized he was a big ol' teddy bear. I remember the day he went to court with me when Tim had gotten into trouble, driving with a suspended license. We sat together in the court room and watched Tim brought in —shackled and hand-cuffed. My heart pounded and my stomach churned. I was petrified at what could happen; but, having my former father-in-law at my side gave me courage and I was grateful. I knew he was there for Tim and not for me; but, his presence was as welcome as a warm blanket on a cold day. When the judge announced what the bail would be and that Tim would be taken to Bridgeport Correctional Facility if bail wasn't posted, tears welled up in my eyes. When we stood up, my legs felt weak and shaky. My father-in-law took me by the arm and we walked out. A bail bondsman approached us. I shook my head and said I had no money. Bail wouldn't be posted. But, Dad put up his hand and said no. He didn't want to see his grandson hauled off to jail. He took care of it. In a short time, Tim was released into our care. This was only a fraction of the turmoil that our family had gone through that year. It's detailed more completely in my first book. But, my father-in-law had played a role that would not be forgotten by Tim nor by me.

As I drove up I-81 North, tears stung my eyes. Several friends had told me that they didn't know if they would have the resolve to go to a funeral in another state and put themselves into an emotional situation with former in-laws and a former spouse. But, the Lord spoke to me clearly as I drove. It was the right thing to do. Immediately, a picture came to mind.

I was reminded of a theory that I heard many years ago that if one would open the windows in the house as a tornado bears down that it would equalize pressure building up and thus save the house from being blown apart. It's the opposite in a hurricane. Homeowners need to board up windows to protect the glass as it's pummeled by the winds. Well, scientists have long since proved that while the theory seems plausible, the force of the churning winds is what blows the house apart not the dynamic change in air-pressure. But, the picture stuck in my mind and I realized that the Lord was showing me an analogy for life.

Let's say the back doors and windows represent our past and the front door and windows represent our future. The inside of our home represents the present time. If we open the door to our past and open the door to our future at the same time, we equalize the pressure of life; in other words, we allow the winds of the Holy Spirit to move through our lives (the present). If we keep the doors and windows to the past tightly shut and are afraid to open the doors and windows of the future, the present time is blown apart by confusion, fear, and turmoil. There is no opportunity for healing. But, when the doors and windows are open, all of them, a cooling, healing wind can pass through. The healing wind carries the Gifts of the Holy Spirit and we must be open to them, not closed.

The revelation came to me and I knew this was where the *courage* would come from to go back. Courage is a Gift of Holy Spirit. Being with my ex-husband and his family was very emotional for me, not only because of the death of a loved one, but, because I found myself with people I've loved and from whom I've been separated. I saw Ed's best man from our wedding. I saw a couple that were a part of our close circle of friends when we first married. Plus, I saw all of Ed's relatives. Despite the emotion, I was so glad to be there with them, to mourn with them and to offer my sympathy. I was so proud of my children at the funeral. Carissa and Timothy conducted themselves with poise and maturity. It was gratifying to see them as adults, despite the ups and downs of the past. God had brought them through it all.

Since that unexpected trip to Connecticut, I have thought many times about the picture that the Lord showed me on my journey. So many people cannot enjoy their present lives because they have been wounded by events from the past. These wounds have crippled them in a sense and threaten to deprive them of a future of hope. So, my prayer for everyone today is to open your doors and windows and let the Holy Spirit touch you and heal you. Don't let pressure build up in your life and combust in an explosion of anger, pain, heartache, misery and so forth.

Our Lord Jesus Christ came so that we might have life. He has delivered us. Accept His love and allow His Holy Spirit to dwell within you, heal you and bring you hope for your future.

*"Everyone who sees the Son and believes in him may have eternal life,
and I shall raise him [on] the last day."*
John 6:40

*May all the words written here bring praise and glory to Jesus Christ
and may His abundant blessings be upon all those who accept Him as
their Lord and Savior. For those of you who have never opened your
heart to Jesus, pray these words with me now,
Lord Jesus, come into my life. Forgive me for my sins.
I believe that you are the
True Son of God, the Messiah, the Holy One,
the Prince of Peace. I know that You
Died on the Cross for our Salvation. Thank you,
Lord, for your sacrifice for me.
I accept the guidance of your Holy Spirit, today and every day.
In Jesus' name.
Amen.*